A NEW DAY DAWNING

A NEW DAY DAWNING

Julie Ellis

This first world edition published in Great Britain 2006 by
SEVERN HOUSE PUBLISHERS LTD of
9–15 High Street, Sutton, Surrey SM1 1DF.
This first world edition published in the USA 2006 by
SEVERN HOUSE PUBLISHERS INC of
595 Madison Avenue, New York, N.Y. 10022.

British Library Cataloguing in Publication Data

Ellis, Julie, 1933-
   A new day dawning
   1.   Women journalists - Fiction
   2.   Arab Americans - Fiction
   3.   Racism - Fiction
   4.   Romantic suspense novels
   I.   Title
   813.5'4 [F]

   ISBN-13: 978-0-7278-6431-4
   ISBN-10: 0-7278-6431-9

All Severn House titles are printed on acid-free paper.

Typeset by Palimpsest Book Production Ltd.,
Polmont, Stirlingshire, Scotland.
Printed and bound in Great Britain by
MPG Books Ltd., Bodmin, Cornwall.

One

On the warm, sunlit morning of September 11th, Karen Hunter lay back against the pillows in the queen-size bed she shared with Gregory Ames and felt herself encased in euphoria. In five days, she and Greg would be married on the beach at Montauk.

They'd moved into this lovely apartment in the Gramercy Park area of Manhattan on the first of the month.

'Why pay rent on our old apartments when we have this one now?' Greg had said.

She'd been shocked at the huge rent they were paying on the new apartment, but Greg had just received a large salary increase. And she loved living high in the sky, with a glorious view of Gramercy Park and much of Lower Manhattan – all the way down to the Twin Towers of the World Trade Center.

She smiled tenderly as Greg's voice in song – slightly off-key – floated from the bathroom. Greg was the best thing that had happened to her in her 31 years. Warm, sweet, funny. He made her feel safe, secure. He made her laugh. He gave her the self-confidence that had so long eluded her.

For almost ten years – since her disastrous break-up with Doug – she'd avoided any romantic relationship, fearful of facing desperate hurt again. So quickly Greg had convinced her that this would be different – a relationship to cherish.

Oh, it was silly of her to lie in bed this way! She should

be dressing for the office. So she'd had a 24-hour virus – which had hit Greg last week. No reason for her not to go into the office this morning. Even if she felt a little dragged out.

She tossed aside the coverlet, felt about for her slippers under her side of the bed.

'Hey, where do you think you're going?' Wrapped in a bath towel, Greg emerged from the bathroom. 'Stay in bed this morning, relax. The office will survive without you today.' She had risen from administrative assistant to junior marketing director in the same firm where Greg was on his way towards a major promotion.

'I feel guilty,' she admitted but resumed her prone position. Greg made her feel so loved, so pampered.

'You should have asked for this week off, too.' He leaned forward for a quick kiss before he began to dress. They were taking two weeks off for their honeymoon – in a borrowed house in Montauk. 'You need your rest. The bride is supposed to be radiant on her wedding day.'

'I ought to at least make your breakfast.' *Life could never be better than this.*

'No.' Greg paused, one leg in his trousers. His expressive face telling her how much she was loved. 'I want to leave home with the vision of you lolling in bed – and thinking of me.' She sensed his surge of passion. 'No,' he decreed with a poignant smile. 'I can't afford to be late for the office. Not when I'm in line for a big promotion in six months.'

In a matter of minutes Greg had left the apartment. She lay back against the pillows and thought about the years ahead with Greg. He wanted a family. So did she. And she agreed with Greg that she would be a stay-at-home mom until their kids were in school. Greg had their whole lives planned. It was an image she cherished.

She knew he was hurt that his parents objected to his marrying her. They'd complained she and Greg had only known each other for four months. Not expecting rejection, Greg had put her on an extension when he called to tell them he was marrying her in mid-September.

'Greg, are you out of your mind?' his father had stormed. 'You can't marry some girl you've known only a few weeks.'

'Four months – and it's as though we've known each other all our lives.'

She was a nobody in their eyes. They were a prominent Massachusetts family. Greg had gone to an Ivy League college, earned his MBA at a prestigious school. She'd gone to a state college – the bastion of the middle-class.

Before she came along, Greg had been seeing the daughter of close friends of his parents. Someone they considered socially acceptable. They were affronted by the knowledge that she was four years Greg's senior. He was hurt – but also furious.

'Their attitude is gross! This is the twenty-first century! My parents can't rule my life.'

Greg hadn't expected them to be so angry as to refuse to attend their wedding. Nor had she.

'We don't need them there,' he'd insisted. 'There'll just be us, the minister and Frank and Michelle.'

Karen's father had died in a hit-and-run accident the beginning of her senior year at college – and three months later her mother, declaring she couldn't cope, had committed suicide. Frank and Michelle were the couple who'd introduced them. Both were colleagues of Greg's – both in more exalted positions than her.

Without any such intention she drifted off into semi-slumber, relishing the luxury of not racing into the office midweek. She was jolted into wakefulness by the insistent ringing of the bedside telephone. She reached to pick up. A glance at the clock on the night table told her it was 8:49 a.m.

'Honey, I wanted you to know I'm all right.' Greg's voice came to her with an unnatural undercurrent of urgency.

'Something crazy is happening. One World Trade Center was just hit by an airliner!' Greg's office was at Two World Trade Center. 'It's on fire! We can smell the smoke – and the fumes of fuel. We may have to evacuate this building. No,' he added swiftly. 'The public address system just announced the building is safe. Karen, I love you—'

'I love you, too.' *What does he mean? One World Trade Center was just hit by an airliner.* 'Greg—' The phone had gone dead.

In a burst of terror, Karen left the bed, darted into the living room, flipped on the TV.

'At 8:45 a.m. – just three minutes ago – a 767 – presumed to have been hijacked – slammed into the north side of One World Trade Center.' The TV commentator was struggling to appear poised. 'The Tower is in flames. Fire trucks, ambulances, emergency crews are rushing to the scene.'

Karen rushed back into the south-facing bedroom, stared out the sweeping picture window. Enveloped in sickening horror, she saw the exploding Tower. She clutched for the support of the heating/air-conditioning unit below the window.

We're being attacked? How can this be happening in this country? Why did Greg's phone go dead? He's not in One World Trade Center.

Dress, go down there, make sure Greg's all right. Why would the second tower be evacuated? At first he said it might . . .

She rushed into slacks and a tee shirt, slid her feet into sneakers – all the while listening to the harrowing report from the TV newsman. By 9 a.m. she was at the elevator, cursing its slowness in arriving. She emerged from the elevator to hear the sounds of the small TV set the concierge kept in his cubicle. He looked up as she approached. Ashen, he pointed to the screen.

'Another plane just hit the second tower! Oh, my God!' For an instant he was speechless in shock. 'Look at that

4

orange ball of fire! How can those people escape? People are jumping from almost a hundred floors up!'

Greg's in the second tower! On a high floor! Let him be all right. Dear God, let him be all right . . .

In the colonial mansion that had been the Ames's home for almost thirty years, Doris Ames sat at her elegant writing table and wrote invitations to a dinner party two weeks hence. She sipped at intervals from the cup of coffee her housekeeper had brought to her as usual at precisely 9 a.m.

The phone rang. She grimaced in annoyance. Elvira – her housekeeper – had gone to the market. *Who was so gauche as to call at this unearthly hour? Let the answering machine pick up.*

Impatient for the machine to provide its service, she waited through the four rings and then the message delivered by her husband. Now her closest friend's voice filtered into the room in shrill tones.

'Doris, have you got your TV on? I can't believe what's happening down in New York! Didn't you tell me that Gregory's firm is located in the World Trade Center?'

With sudden anxiety Doris reached for the phone. 'Martha, what are you mumbling about? What's happened at the World Trade Center?' As she listened, her face drained of color, while Martha reported on the horror that had descended on Lower Manhattan. 'I have to call Clark,' Doris interrupted. 'This is insane!'

She dialed her husband's private line at his investment banking firm. His executive secretary picked up.

'This is Doris Ames. I must talk to my husband immediately.'

'He's in an important meeting,' Clark Ames' secretary began. 'There's some dreadful trouble down in New York City—'

'I know,' Doris broke in urgently. 'Did Clark forget that Greg works at the World Trade Center? Get him to the phone.'

Moments later his voice came to her with that constrained calm that told her he was aware that Greg might be in serious danger.

'I didn't call you just yet because I wanted to learn more about what was happening. You know there're two towers down there.'

'You haven't been listening to the TV,' she shot back. 'The second one has been attacked! Clark, we have to fly down there immediately!'

'Every plane in the country has been grounded.' He hesitated. 'I planned to come home as soon as I had some information about traveling.'

'Come now,' she commanded. 'I don't care if we have to walk, we're going to New York. Don't you realize our son may be trapped in one of those burning buildings?'

Karen dashed from the apartment, signaled to a taxi driver at the curb to wait for her. She was grateful he'd just deposited a passenger here. The passenger – obviously aware of what was happening in Lower Manhattan – hurried past her with a brief, silent exchange of anguish.

Normally the subway would have been faster – but the newscaster had reported that all trains had stopped running. She hurried into the taxi, gave the driver her destination.

'Lady, nobody wants to go down to the World Trade Center now,' he gasped. 'I don't think the police will let us through.'

'I have to go there.' She fought for breath, reached into her purse for a large bill, held it out to him. 'Take me as close as you can get.'

The sounds of police sirens, racing ambulances, fire trucks filled the air as the taxi crept southward. Police officers seemed everywhere – directing traffic to allow passage of emergency vehicles. Karen clenched her hands until the nails broke skin. The driver reached to switch on his car radio as they stalled in traffic yet again.

'A 757 just slammed into the Pentagon! The White House is being evacuated.'

At Union Square the taxi driver pulled to a stop at the directions of a traffic cop.

'Lady, this is as far as we can go. The cops won't let us go any further.' He spread his hands in a gesture of futility.

Karen left the taxi, joined the mass of pedestrians on the long walk to the horror scene. People clutched cell phones, frantic to reach relatives or friends in the madness below. But there were no signals to be had.

Were people escaping those twin infernos? Greg had talked about evacuating his building – but then he said an announcement came over the public address system. *They were supposed to be safe.* But that was before the second plane rammed into Two World Trade Center, she realized. Greg's building. He'd always been so pleased at being close to the top. He loved the views. She shuddered, felt sick remembering what the television screen had shown the world as it was happening.

The elevators couldn't be used, she thought – her throat tight with fear. How long would it take Greg – and all the others on high floors – to walk down nearly a hundred flights? She felt sick at the vision of thousands of people trying to escape down the stairs of the Twin Towers

Fire trucks and ambulances continued to scream as they made their way toward the disaster scene. Karen fought against dizziness. Her feet ached as she trudged towards her destination. The ominous smoke spiraling into the sky her guide. Pushing her way forward along with countless others.

Where's Greg? Has he escaped that burning inferno? How will I find him in the midst of this madness?

Two

Karen was mesmerized by the sight of the two smoking towers – with gaping holes – that loomed terrifyingly close. The aroma of smoke irritated her throat. How long had she been walking? An hour? How long did it take to walk down almost a hundred flights of stairs?

An army of fire trucks, ambulances and utility vans permeated the area. Karen caught her breath as she watched people in various states emerge from the lobbies of the twin towers. She strained for some familiar sign that said one of those was Greg.

People were coming out, she told herself with relief – trying to banish from her mind the visions shown on television. People jumping – or falling – from high floors. Greg was bright – he was strong. He would know how to escape.

Some were moving as though in shock – with no apparent destination. Those who had made their way out of the burning buildings, she interpreted. Some bloodied, limping. Some silently sobbing. Crews rushed to carry the seriously injured to ambulances. Instinct warned Karen this was dangerous territory – but like so many others she lingered here.

'Move uptown!' The voices of police officers rang out through the odd quiet. 'The buildings could fall. Move north – it's not safe here!'

But no one left. They remained – galvanized. Each seeking a loved one, a friend who'd been in those infernos. *Where's Greg? Is he all right? How can I find him here?*

Then all at once a horrendous noise splintered the still-ness. In disbelief, the thousands gathered here watched the structure that had been One World Trade Center begin to shake. It listed in one direction. How could something so tall, so awesome, fall?

The tower began to collapse – bursting inward, falling floor by floor, second by second. Screams filled the air. Darkness was descending on the area.

'Karen!'

Karen was conscious of a familiar feminine voice, then felt herself being pulled to the ground, tugged beneath a truck.

'Jackie—' Karen whispered. A receptionist in her office. 'Are you all right?' Even in the darkness, she saw the gaping wound on Jackie's forehead.

'When it's safe to get out from here,' Jackie gasped, 'I'll go to the medics.'

'Have you seen Greg?' Karen's voice was a tortured whisper.

Jackie was silent. Karen's heart began to pound.

'Jackie, tell me. Did he get out of the building?'

'He went back to help Elise – she was hysterical.' Jackie paused. 'I was one of the last to get out. Karen – I don't think he made it.'

'He made it,' Karen insisted. She wouldn't believe anything else. 'I'll find him.'

The south tower was disappearing in a cloud of ash. Smoke rose upward as though an atomic bomb had been dropped, to fall moments later to the street. The two women – like others around them – crept out of their momentary refuge. The darkness began to clear.

'You need care.' Karen fought for composure. *Greg's all right. I know he is.*

'I have to call my mom—' Jackie began to sway.

Karen reached out to her. 'Let me help you.'

A medic appeared, lifted Jackie from her feet.

'She'll be okay,' he said, carrying her towards one of the improvised emergency medical stations.

Karen stood immobile, trying to digest what Jackie had told her. Jackie doesn't know – she's just surmising.

Amid the screams came cries of warning. 'Try not to breathe! The air may be toxic!'

Many covered with ash and plaster dust, people ran northward, then – hypnotized by the horror – paused at a distance to gaze backward. Gaped – numb – at the empty space where once had stood One World Trade Center.

Karen groped for a tissue. Her eyes felt as though on fire. Her throat hurt. Breathing labored. Around her she saw others covering their faces with whatever was available.

'Get out before the other tower falls!' a man yelled.

Moments later, more eruptions, one after another in swift succession. Again massive smoke clouds darkened the area. The second tower was collapsing. People ran in fresh alarm. The smoke followed, beginning to dissipate at last at Canal Street.

Along with countless others, Karen abandoned running, gaped at the warped, steel girders that were all that remained of the Twin Towers. A heavy white ash was settling on the ground. Beside her a man wept in disbelief. A woman close by cried hysterically.

How could this have happened in America? It was as though the whole world had stopped, Karen thought. As though there could be no tomorrow.

A woman close by was trying to put a call through on her cell phone, tried repeatedly. Maybe Greg had tried to call her again – Karen seized at this possibility. Perhaps there was a message on her machine. She pushed forward along with others. Her eyes searched for a pay phone.

A few phones appeared to be working – but the lines were endless. Go home, Karen ordered herself. Fresh hope spiraled in her. Greg would want to go home, to reassure her. With renewed strength she walked north.

Around her others were gathering in clusters to try to comprehend what was happening. Some huddled about cars where drivers had switched on radios – blaring the news of the horror that had hit Lower Manhattan and the Pentagon. Except for emergency vehicles, traffic was startlingly light. Most shops had closed.

'Hey, they need blood at the hospitals,' a man called out. 'It just came over the radio.'

Karen glanced up at the street sign – she was at East 13th Street. Only a few blocks from home. But those few blocks seemed miles now. She spied a cab up ahead. It was about to disgorge a passenger. She pushed her way through the still dazed throng – seeming uncertain now about any real destination.

'Taxi!' she called, breathless from the effort. 'Wait. Please wait.'

She climbed inside, gave the driver her destination. Had he heard her? He seemed to focus on the voice from the radio. He pulled away from the curb, paused almost immediately because a trio of ambulances were speeding down the avenue.

At East 15th he stopped for a red light. A tall, burly man in shorts – his arm bandaged from shoulder to wrist – leaned forward menacingly. 'You an Arab?' he demanded.

'What's it to you?' the driver shot back.

'Because if you're an Arab, you're dead!'

'I'm Indonesian,' the driver mumbled in shock. 'I been in this country almost ten years.'

'Okay.' The other man nodded in approval. 'You're okay.'

Karen saw the driver's hands trembling on the wheel. Only now did she stop to consider who was responsible for what had happened here and in Washington. Terrorists from an Arab country. Probably some fanatic.

Karen focused on what the radio newscaster was reporting. Planes throughout the country were grounded. President Bush had flown west from Florida. Vice-President

Cheney was in a bunker – running the government. Over 300,000 government workers had been evacuated in Washington.

'Okay, lady.' The still visibly shaken driver turned to her. 'You're here.'

'Thanks.' Karen reached into her purse, found bills, gave them to the driver.

Not waiting for change she darted across the sidewalk and into the building. Jim, the concierge, still sat glued to his small TV set – as when she'd left.

'Jim . . .' Karen paused, fearful. 'Has Greg come home?'

Wordless – his eyes revealing his alarm – Jim shook his head. 'Not yet . . .'

She raced to the elevator, waited with soaring impatience for it to descend. It zoomed down to the lobby without stopping at any floors. Her heart pounding, she rushed inside. Maybe Greg had to stay down there to do something for the firm. He was super-conscientious. But he would have left a message on the answering machine.

She fumbled in her purse, found her keys. Swore under her breath because of her awkwardness with the two locks that were standard in Manhattan apartments. There, it was open. She ran into the living room, a hand reaching out in readiness to push the message button on the answering machine.

'You have one message,' the recorded voice reported. 'I will play one new message.'

Exhausted, light-headed, she waited. But the only sounds that emerged were the odd noises that told her a tele-marketer had left no message because that was a waste of time. No news from Greg.

He's all right. He's got to be all right. He's still down there – he's trying to help. Should I go back, try to find him? No, I have to be here when he comes home. I have to be here if he phones.

*   *   *

Doris Ames paced about her living room, waiting for her husband to be off the phone.

'Well?' she demanded when he put down the receiver. 'Are we to drive to Boston for the train?' Hours wasted, she fumed.

'No trains are running into New York City.' Clark Ames stared into space. 'No planes – but you know that already.'

'What about a bus?' she persisted. 'I know it's a long haul, but let's drive.'

He shook his head. 'Doris, New York City is isolated from the rest of the world. The bridges, the tunnels are closed. Even some of the highways leading into the city. Doris, we have to wait until we can fly.' He shuddered. 'Perhaps we should take a train – as soon as they're running into New York.'

'When will that be?' Her voice was shrill with fear. 'I have to hear from my son!'

'Amtrak will probably be running tomorrow,' he soothed. 'I'll keep checking.'

Doris hesitated. 'What about that girl he's seeing? Do you suppose she might know something?'

'How would we find her?' Clark countered. 'We don't even know where she lives.'

'You know her name,' Doris shrieked. 'Call information. Get her phone number. Call her!'

For almost an hour Clark tried to get through to Karen.

'It's useless,' he conceded. Fighting for control. 'Half the country's trying to get through to New York. We'll have to wait. We may be able to get a train from Boston in the morning.'

Three

Karen sat huddled on a corner of the sofa for hours. Her eyes were fastened on the television screen. Mayor Giuliani had earlier ordered an evacuation of Manhattan south of Canal Street. UN headquarters had been evacuated. Along with workers in the two buildings, many firemen, policemen, rescue workers were feared dead.

Where is Greg? Why doesn't he call me?

At moments rage blended with anxiety. Didn't Greg know how terrified she was? She yearned to rush downtown again, yet logic told her she must remain by the phone. *Jackie's wrong – Greg got out of the building in time.* A TV newscaster quoted Mayor Giuliani: 'The number of casualties will be more than any of us can bear ultimately, and I don't think we want to speculate on the number of casualties.'

The phone rang. Joy surged in her. She reached to reply. 'Hello, darling!'

'It's me – Jackie.' Pain in her voice. 'They stitched up my cut at the hospital and sent me home with a sedative. The stitches will come out in five days.' Jackie paused, took an audible breath. 'I – I managed to get in touch with somebody from the company. Karen, it's bad. They figure we lost a lot of people.'

'They don't know!' Karen rejected. 'How can they know at this point?'

'It will be days before we know,' Jackie acknowledged. 'Days . . .' Her voice trailed off.

14

A New Day Dawning

'They said on TV that a lot of people are going to hospitals around the city – even in Jersey. To check on lists of those being brought in.' Karen clung to this with stubborn hope. 'Maybe some haven't been identified yet – they're in shock.'

'Do you want to go to the hospitals?' Jackie asked. 'Would you like me to go with you?'

'I'll wait here another hour,' Karen said after a moment. 'Can you come over here?' All at once she dreaded being alone. 'Please?'

'It'll take me a while – I have to walk from East 39th Street,' Jackie reminded her. 'But I'll be there.'

Karen alternated between watching the horror on TV and gazing out of her living room window for sight of Jackie. She needed the comfort of Jackie's presence. Jackie had been there in the building with Greg. She'd seen him after the plane hit.

With a sudden compulsion, Karen strode into the bedroom, crossed to the window wall facing south. *Greg is down there somewhere. People are talking about air pockets – the malls – where those trapped might still be alive.*

She reached to close the drapes against the night, stopped herself. *I can't close the drapes – it would be as though I'm closing out Greg.* Once again she gazed out into the night and saw where the Twin Towers used to be.

In a spurt of restlessness she returned to the living room, resumed her vigil at the window that looked down on the street. Later, she spied Jackie approaching the entrance to the building, and darted to open her apartment door. She heard the elevator gliding upward. It slid to a stop. Jackie emerged – pale, in fresh wardrobe, a bandage across her forehead.

'Mom's a nervous wreck,' Jackie said, walking to the door. 'I told her I'd be sleeping over with you tonight – but I'll call her every three or four hours.' She searched Karen's face. 'Have you eaten?'

15

Karen shuddered. 'How can I eat?'

'I know. But Mom sat me down at the table and wouldn't let me leave until I ate a sandwich.'

'I can't eat.' Karen's eyes shot back to the TV screen. 'I just want to find Greg.'

'Okay, we'll try the hospitals. There're long lines, I hear – but they have lists. We might as well start now.' Jackie's eyes told Karen that she was convinced Greg would neither phone nor walk into the apartment.

'All right. But let me leave a new message on the answering machine – for Greg. Just in case . . .'

For endless hours they trudged – beside hordes of others with hope and fear in their eyes – from one hospital to another. The city seemed a ghost town. Shops closed, offices idled, little traffic. But Greg's name appeared on no lists.

It was close to midnight by the time Karen and Jackie returned to the apartment. Both exhausted, sick with anxiety and uncertainty. Jackie called her mother, then both retired for the night – yearning for the temporary release of sleep yet suspecting it would be elusive. Karen on the recliner, Jackie on the sofa.

By dawn, Karen and Jackie sat again before the television set. Their sleep had been disrupted by nightmares.

'I ask myself if I'll ever be able to sleep again,' Jackie whispered in anguish as they listened to the television reports. 'I'm afraid to sleep – to live through it all again.'

'I feel guilty that I wasn't there with Greg. I should have been there,' Karen rebuked herself.

'Don't ever think that!' Jackie closed her eyes for a moment. 'I'll never forget climbing down those endless stairs – stepping over sections of walls, broken glass, puddles of water. It took us almost an hour to get down.' Now Jackie was talking with a compulsive need to share. 'I can still hear the screaming, the crying, the praying. I don't think any of us truly expected to get out. All those floors – we were exhausted, fighting for strength to go

16

on. We were climbing down – and the firemen were climbing up. They were wonderful. So many firemen and cops dead now . . .'

But Greg is out there somewhere. In shock, amnesiac. How can I find him?

Towards morning newscasters reported about the 'Missing' posters that were springing up on lamp posts, empty storefronts, stretches of wall space.

While Jackie – insisting they must eat – prepared break-fast, Karen sat again before the TV set. There were phone numbers for employees of various companies to call for information.

'Jackie!' Karen called. Hope springing alive again. 'We can call the company! They may know about Greg!'

But there was no real news, they discovered. So many people were thought to have been lost.

'Why don't they mention names?' Karen harangued. Praying Greg's would not be among them. 'So they expect to reopen somewhere in Westchester. I won't go back. Not until Greg's found. How could I go back?'

'Karen.' Jackie dropped to the edge of the sofa. Her eyes anguished. 'I – I think I should tell you . . .'

'Tell me what?'

'About what happened when the plane hit us.' Jackie took a deep breath. 'I told you I saw Greg trying to convince Elise to leave. They were standing by the windows. There was another explosion – and – and then I didn't see them anymore. That's when somebody grabbed me by the arm and pulled me towards the stairwell.'

'Greg got out,' Karen insisted. 'He's missing – but he got out.'

Karen – accompanied by Jackie – joined the frenzied parade of people invading the copy centers around the city – those that were open. She had letter-sized 'Missing' posters made up with Greg's photo and vital statistics. She searched her mind for what he had been wearing yesterday morning, for minute details of identification. She remembered the tiny scar just above his eyebrow – sustained when he was a toddler at a playground.

All at once avenues of photos of the missing appeared everywhere. One next to the other in an endless display. At the Armory at 26th Street and Lexington streams of people lined up to list their missing.

On Thursday Karen went out – along with many others – and ordered more posters, taped them up in more areas. Strangers walked along the streets and cried silently at the parade of the missing. Thursday afternoon Jackie explained she'd have to go back home.

'Mom's getting paranoid. I have to go home, let her see I'm okay.' She paused in thought. 'Karen, I'll never again work in a tall office building. Never!'

Late Thursday evening while Karen sat before the television set – seeing once again the grim statistics about the missing – her intercom rang. Hope surging, she hurried to respond.

'Yes?'

'There's a Mr and Mrs Ames here,' the concierge reported uncomfortably. 'They're asking for the keys to their son's apartment.'

Karen paused in shock. They didn't know she was here. 'Send them up.'

They didn't realize she'd moved in with Greg. But then they had refused to recognize her as their prospective daughter-in-law. Bracing herself for a strained confrontation, she went to the door to await their arrival.

She heard the elevator come to a stop on her floor. The door slid open. A visibly distraught woman was striding towards her. Greg's father followed. She recognized them from a snapshot Greg had shown her.

'Have you heard from my son?' Doris Ames asked as she approached Karen.

'No,' Karen whispered. 'He's missing . . .' The posters had made her accept this.

'He didn't tell us you had moved in together.' Clark Ames made it sound an affront.

'We didn't see the point of my paying another month's rent when we were to be married in two weeks.' Karen pulled the door wide, gesturing for them to enter. *How can I talk about such mundane things when Greg is missing?* 'I've checked out all the hospitals. He wasn't there. He's officially listed as missing . . .' Her throat tightened. 'It – it's been awful, not knowing.'

'I have connections with the firm.' Clark Ames cleared his throat. 'When we found it impossible to get into Manhattan on Tuesday, I made phone calls – when it was possible to get calls through. I was told that Greg was listed among the missing.'

'We came to the city to close up his apartment, take his things home with us.' Doris's voice was unsteady. Her eyes scolded Karen for being alive.

'It's just three days,' Karen stammered.

'There's no way Greg could have escaped. That was made clear to me.' His father's voice brusque – from grief, Karen told herself. 'There'll be no remains.'

'Greg said you worked with him at his office.' Doris seemed to be forcing the admission that she was aware of Karen's presence in Greg's life 'But you're here.'

Karen flinched before the rage she saw in Doris Ames' eyes. 'I'd had a virus. Greg insisted I stay home on Tuesday . . .' Greg had saved her life.

'When will you be out of our son's apartment?' Clark Ames asked.

'I – I don't know.' Karen struggled for composure.

'Think about it,' Doris ordered. 'Within a week,' she stipulated after a moment. 'Leave the keys with the concierge.'

'And Greg's car?' his father picked up.

Shaken but suddenly defiant, Karen gazed from Clark

Ames to his wife, back to Clark. They wanted to strip her of every tie to Greg – as though their four months together had never existed. 'Greg had no car.' The new car he'd bought just last week was registered in her name. '*Your engagement present.*' She'd gone with him when he'd bought the car. He'd been eager to know she approved of the color. The salesman had gaped in astonishment when Greg handed him his mastercard. '*I've never sold a car for cash before.*'

'Greg has always had a car.' His mother brought Karen back to the moment. 'Ever since he had a driver's license.'

'He doesn't now. Would you care to see my registration?' Her eyes defied them.

'We'll discuss this with the garage people downstairs.' Doris turned to her husband. 'Clark, you'll take care of that.'

'Meanwhile, let me show you the registration to my car.' Karen crossed to pick up her purse, pulled out a card case. The car was Greg's gift to her. She'd allow no one to take it away – it was her last link to him. 'This is my registration for the 2001 Camry parked in the downstairs garage. And yes,' she said, fighting a surge of hopelessness. 'I'll be out of here within the week.'

Without a word Greg's parents walked out of the apartment and out her life. She sank into a chair – too numb to cry. Greg lay somewhere beneath the rubble that had been the Twin Towers. He wasn't coming home.

Four

A lone in the apartment, Karen grappled with reality. What was she to do with her life? The whole world had changed on September 11th – and she must cope with this. Without Greg – who'd made life seem beautiful.

She couldn't have stayed on in this apartment – even if Greg's parents hadn't wanted her out. How could she pay the obscene rent? She'd given up her rent-stabilized apartment – which in New York was like a trust fund – to move into 'their' apartment. She'd run into an old neighbor who'd told her it had been re-rented right away – with some window-dressing supplied – at three times what she'd paid.

She closed her eyes and remembered the day Greg told her about his major promotion . . .

'The money's sensational, Karen. We can afford a great new apartment – we won't have to stay in my place. We'll run over and see this pad I just heard about – and if you like it, I'll sign the lease.'

She'd spent most of her life feeling an outsider. With Greg she was somebody. He'd given her the courage to be herself.

'Honey, you're bright and beautiful. And you should nurture this talent God gave you. Go for it, Karen.' When, back in the high-school years, she talked – tentative, self-conscious – to Mom about becoming a journalist, Mom had scoffed. 'Don't be a feather-brain. You'll get your BA – go on for a masters in education. You'll have security in teaching.'

She'd finished college – but there'd been no money to go for a masters. She could have done it at night – lots of students did. But she'd had no incentive.

With fresh pain she remembered how her dad – whom she'd adored – had been killed in a hit-and-run accident early in her senior year. On Christmas Eve Mom had committed suicide. She'd left a note. 'It's too late for me. I can't cope without your father.'

She remembered the horror of settling the family estate. The house which she and Mom had thought was paid off was heavily mortgaged. Only then did she learn of the debts that her father had piled up in his efforts to supply the lifestyle her mother considered her birthright.

Mom had never worked a day in her life. She'd spent her life in an angry haze, Karen realized now. Forever bickering with her older sister and younger brother – until the final breach with both when she herself was seven. 'I was the forgotten child – the middle child. Cynthia was the oldest – and that made her special – and Joel was the baby brother.'

Karen had felt so alone in her growing-up years. Her aunt, her uncle, an assortment of cousins had moved away. She didn't even know where they'd settled. And Mom never liked having people come to the house. Fishing trips had been Dad's escape. Every Sunday in fishing season – despite Mom's sarcastic remarks – Dad went fishing. Sometimes he took her along with him. Those were special times.

After Greg came into her life, she felt like a whole person. Now she was alone again – and she didn't dare look more than a few days ahead.

She was without a job – with some money in their joint checking account. Wincing at the need for this, she told herself to close the account first thing in the morning. Before Greg's parents tried to hassle her over even that.

How long before the company found another space, was

set to run? *But how can I work for the company again –
with Greg gone?*

She shivered, remembering what they'd learned when
Jackie called the company number. No names were available – but they suspected most were missing. Out of the
300 staff. How could she go back to an office full of ghosts?

She forced herself to think about the immediate future.
Stay here for another day or two, she decided. Not for the
week that Greg's parents had set as a deadline. She needed
to get away from here – where everything reminded her of
Greg.

Each time her eyes rested on the phone, she had to admit
it would never ring again with Greg at the other end of the
line. She'd sleep tonight on the sofa. She couldn't bear
lying on their bed.

Greg had a wonderful way of making her laugh. Would
she ever laugh again? There had been little laughter in her
life until Greg had come along.

She'd go out to the house in Montauk. Just for a few
days. She couldn't think beyond that right now. She'd walk
on the beach where they were to be married. In tortuous
recall she remembered him saying how one day – in the
distant future, they'd assumed then – he'd like to have his
ashes strewn at the water's edge in Montauk.

And after Montauk? The insidious question crept into her
mind. Where would she go then? Her whole life had come
to center around Greg – after such a short while. Where
would she go after Montauk?

Greg gave her the confidence that had always eluded her.
He'd made her feel less vulnerable. Not doomed to failure.
Mom had always torn her down. Greg made her feel she
could do anything she set out to do. *But Greg is gone –
and my world will never be the same again.*

Determined not to fall apart – because Greg wouldn't
want that to happen – she focused on immediate tasks.
She'd pack her personal possessions, be ready to load them

into the car. Forget what little furniture she'd brought into their new apartment. Each piece would only be a cruel reminder that Greg was forever gone from her life.

Is the key to the Montauk house here? Was Greg carrying it?

In sudden alarm she rushed into the bedroom to search for it. If Greg didn't have the key on him, then it would be in the drawer of the night table beside their bed. That's where he kept any important papers. 'Until we have a decent desk,' he'd said.

Now, the realization that Michelle and Frank were among the missing assaulted her. No one answered the phone – there was only Michelle's perky voice asking the caller to leave a message and phone number. Finally – today – dreading what she might hear, she'd been able to get a call through to Michelle's sister.

'There was no way Michelle and Frank could have gotten out.'

Michelle's sister's voice had been drained of emotion. She'd put up posters, though she knew there was no chance Michelle and Frank were alive.

'I had to put up "Missing" posters – but Karen, we know. They're gone.'

Karen pulled open the drawer that held their important papers. Cold as ice, she pulled out their marriage license, brought it up to her face. She'd walk along the water's edge at Montauk, say her final good-bye to Greg, and piece by piece let it float out into the Atlantic.

On Friday morning – after a night of waking in fear at every outdoor sound: a fire truck, an ambulance, a car alarm – Karen recoiled from facing another day in New York. Still in her nightgown – her mind darting ahead – she phoned Jackie.

'Hello.' Jackie sounded half-asleep, scared.

'It's me,' Karen said. 'Did I wake you?' she asked in sudden alarm.

'Who sleeps these nights?' Jackie shrugged this off.

A hurried glance at the living-room clock told Karen it was barely 7 a.m.

'I figured I'd call the office number a little later,' Jackie said. 'They're supposed to be looking for space for temporary headquarters.'

'I won't go back!' Karen felt sick at the prospect.

'Karen, you have a good job. It won't be easy to find another one.'

'I'm going out to Montauk for a few days. I don't know where I'll go from there . . .'

She'd leave today, Karen decided.

'Montauk?' Jackie sounded bewildered.

'That's where Greg and I were – were to spend our honeymoon. I have the key to the cottage.' Her voice broke. 'It belongs to Michelle and Frank.'

'Who?' Jackie's voice was puzzled.

'Michelle and Frank, from the office,' she explained. How quickly the horror had brought Jackie and her together. Before, they'd been casual office acquaintances.

She remembered how Jackie talked about the way people helped one another on the nightmare journey down endless flights of stairs to safety. Jackie had said, 'I don't think I would have made it if those two strangers hadn't kept insisting I keep moving.'

She told Jackie about the visit of Greg's parents last night, about her realization that she couldn't remain in the apartment even if she wished to.

'What creeps!' Jackie said, shocked.

'I think I'll leave today.' Karen paused. 'I have to get away.'

'Write down my address,' Jackie urged. 'Keep in touch . . .'

By noon Karen had loaded her possessions into the car. Clothes, books, mementos from earlier years. An insulated bag that they'd used for a beach picnic during the summer, was stuffed with the contents of the refrigerator. How could she be concerned about such things as a time like this? she taunted herself.

She turned over the keys to the concierge, to be collected by Greg's parents. Only one key to the house in Montauk, she thought – but two locks were standard in Manhattan apartments.

'You take care of yourself now,' the concierge said, his eyes exuding sympathy.

'Thanks, I will.' She leaned forward to accept his warm embrace.

Earlier she'd gone to the bank to close out her small savings account, her joint checking account with Greg. Later she'd worry about her pension plan, the IRA.

She was startled to feel a sense of fear as she approached the Queens-Midtown tunnel. Would she ever be able to walk into a tall building, enter a tunnel, cross a bridge without being terrified? She was conscious of the heavy security as she approached the toll booths. Going through, she noted that incoming trucks were being stopped, inspected.

How had America come to this? She remembered what a commentator had said this morning – that America had never felt the invasion of an enemy since 1812, when the Capitol was burned by invading British forces. But these were religious fanatics who hated America, hated the progress it represented.

They hated movies, television, freedom and education for women – culture that the rest of the world took for granted. They were barbarians, intent on making the world over in their image. They took young children and raised them in their ugly philosophy, taught them that to die in killing innocent civilians was to assure themselves a place in Paradise.

Her hands ached from the tautness with which she grasped the wheel. Should she have stayed in Manhattan? Could there be some miracle that would bring Greg back to her? Four mornings ago he stood by their bed and ordered her not to go into the office. Four mornings ago he was the center of her life.

But reason told her to let go of this dream. On Tuesday morning – when that 767 hit the second World Trade Tower – Greg lingered a moment too long at the windows. He'd been blown out to his death.

She flipped on the radio with a need to hear a human voice. The newscaster was issuing statistics about the number of dead. She flinched in recurrent disbelief. Within the space of less than two hours over 5,000 people – the newspapers estimated – had been rendered missing. Like Greg, most of them presumed dead. Hundreds of firemen and policemen among them.

She felt sick as she remembered the rows of faces on the 'Missing' posters that adorned so much space in Manhattan. Most of them young. Husbands, wives, mothers, fathers. How many children robbed of one parent – or even both?

Outgoing traffic was heavier than she'd anticipated. She remembered that September weekends always sent a stream of New Yorkers out to the Hamptons. Perhaps some – like herself – were running away from the ruins that still smoldered four days later.

She'd never felt comfortable driving in heavy traffic. She was impatient to be off the Long Island Expressway. With relief she reached Exit 70, headed towards the strip that would take her to Route 27. Had it been just two weeks ago that she and Greg had driven out to Montauk with Michelle and Frank? It seemed another world ago.

Turning on to Route 27 she was conscious of the abundance of flags that fluttered from many houses. At intervals there were signs: 'We Love America', 'We Shall Overcome.' But how was she to overcome the end of the world she'd so joyously discovered with Greg?

Five

Karen drove into Montauk with some misgivings about directions to the house. Searching her memory she found herself in territory that seemed familiar. And then she saw it. The charming, much-glassed, red cedar contemporary that was to have been their honeymoon house. Its sweeping expanse of deck bathed in sunlight this afternoon – as though the world had not turned upside down.

She turned into the driveway – conscious of the magnificent stretch of blue Atlantic that lay below the house. Later she'd pull into the garage. Right now she'd only carry the valise she'd packed with temporary wardrobe, the insulated bag with food supplies. Tomorrow was a world she couldn't bring herself to face.

She switched on the refrigerator, stored the contents of the insulated bag, and debated about where she'd sleep. She recoiled from sleeping alone in the bedroom she'd shared with Greg just two weeks ago. Not the bedroom that had been Michelle's and Frank's either.

She carried the valise she'd brought up with her into the third bedroom, hung away its contents. For a few days this would be her escape from the world. She kicked off her shoes, slid her feet into sneakers. In a little while she'd walk down the flight of stairs that led to the beach.

She stood at the slider of the bedroom she had expected to share with Greg – almost feeling his presence. Then in sudden impatience she pushed the slider open, walked on to the wraparound deck. How could it seem so normal out here? As though death and destruction had not descended on Lower Manhattan.

She walked across the deck, down the stairs that led to the beach. The first Montauk daisies bursting into flower beside the house. The water rough. Both she and Greg had loved to see the waves crashing onto the beach.

Involuntarily she remembered how Doug – all those years ago – had talked with such affection about the coastline of Maine. She hadn't allowed herself to think of Doug since that painful senior year at college. *Why am I thinking about him now?*

Claire – with whom she'd shared a dorm room during her junior and senior year – was such a romanticist. She always insisted every woman always remembered her first love.

'I don't mean the 11-year-old crush,' Claire conceded. 'But your high-school sweetheart – or college love. They're always there in a corner of your heart.'

She'd made a determined effort – after a few months of believing herself forever in love with Doug – to thrust him from her mind. The hurt, the shock he'd brought into that frenetic senior year – on top of the deaths of her parents – had been buried in her search for a new life.

And here I am again – in search of a new life. I've bombed out twice with the men in my life. Maybe it's time to realize I'm meant to go it alone.

She forced herself to focus on the beauty of glistening blue water as she walked along the beach – deserted except for a sprinkling of seagulls. The sand untouched by footprints – only the imprints of tiny seagull feet. With a painful twinge she recalled the last weekend she and Greg had spent here with Michelle and Frank – the way they'd brought a loaf of bread along at Michelle's insistence.

'We can't come down to the beach without throwing crumbs to the gulls,' Michelle had said.

But Michelle and Frank would never walk here again.

Now pain was replaced by rage as faces of others in the office darted across her mind. Jackie said many were listed among the missing. All their families never to be the same again.

She felt herself grow hot with anger. How could this happen in a country like theirs? She paused at the edge of the water and gazed without seeing at the horizon. Instead, she saw the shrines that stood in front of the fire stations, the crayon drawings by children who never should have been exposed to such horror, the melted-down candles at the shrine in Union Square.

She – who couldn't bring herself to step on an ant – could stand by and watch these mass murderers mutilated until they were dead.

Karen walked until she was exhausted, then turned back and climbed the flight of stairs to the house. She dragged a chaise out on to the deck, and dropped along its length. In moments – lulled by the lush breeze from the Atlantic – she was asleep.

She awoke with a start – in the fear evoked by every unexpected sound since the attack on Manhattan. A car alarm, she realized – even in this lovely, earlier-world town. She was aware now that the sun was going down. A rosy hue filled the sky. How long had she slept?

The sound of music in the next house told her that weekenders were arriving. Out here, she thought with simmering resentment, it was as though nothing had happened. And yet in the back of her mind she knew there was not one corner of America – few corners in the world – where the horror of Tuesday morning was not felt.

She was astonished to be conscious of hunger. With a reluctance to leave the seascape before her, she went into the house. She'd have a sandwich and a cup of tea. She'd brought cheese and bread from the New York apartment, boxes of tea. How strange to feel hunger at the same time as pain.

But, moving about the kitchen – where such a little while ago she and Michelle had prepared dinner for Greg and Frank and themselves – she asked herself if she had been wise to come out here. To this house of ghosts. Yet in some odd way she felt close to Greg here.

She noted a chill in the air as she settled herself in the ocean-facing living room with her grilled cheese sandwich and tea. She remembered how Greg had started a fire in the grate their last time here. Logs sat in readiness beside the fireplace. On sudden impulse she ignored her sandwich to start a fire. She lingered on her haunches until flames spiraled from the logs and the room was filled with the aroma of birch.

She ate without tasting. Lost in thought. For four months she'd shared a piece of paradise with Greg. He'd been so good to her, she thought yet again. So good for her. She'd realized right off that his relationship with his family was not good. He'd been looking for something to give his life meaning. They'd been so good for each other.

What she'd felt for Greg, she analyzed with new candor, was not the tumultuous love she'd felt for Doug. It was something more real – built on a stronger foundation. But where did she go from here?

She sat far into the night on the living-room sofa. Drapes wide across the wall of sliders that brought the ocean indoors. The only light the glow from the fireplace, which she fed until the logs were down to embers.

A light blanket about her against the night chill, she slept at intervals on the sofa. Waking hourly until dawn until heavy slumber overtook her.

She awoke with a start. Daylight streamed into the room. What time was it? She glanced at her watch. Past 7 a.m. Only now did she realize she'd never retired for the night. She was still dressed from the day before.

She'd remembered, she thought gratefully, to turn on the hot water when she first arrived. She'd need a hot shower

31

to become fully awake. What to do with today? Shower and go over to that charming restaurant where they'd had breakfast each time the four of them had come out during the summer. But first she'd walk on the beach – and float her marriage certificate out to sea.

Karen sat with her marriage certificate in her hands for endless minutes. She hated the monsters who'd destroyed her life and so many others with an intensity that startled her. A person who had loathed the existence of capital punishment, now she ached to see these murderers dead. Let the government go over there – to that Middle Eastern country where the newspapers said they had their camps to train other terrorists in their own images – and annihilate them.

At last she forced herself to leave the house, walk down the stairs to the early-morning-deserted beach and across the sand to the sun-kissed waves. So rough this morning, she thought – as though they knew the turmoil in her heart.

While a pair of seagulls cawed noisily over the waves, she dropped to her haunches, folded the marriage license into a paper boat and launched it on outgoing waves. There went her tomorrow.

With a compulsive need for action she began to walk along the empty beach. Now she saw a lone figure trudging towards her. As the other woman approached, she waved a hand in greeting. She smiled but her eyes were somber.

'It's a beautiful morning,' she greeted Karen. 'Walking along the beach it's hard to realize what happened Tuesday morning . . .'

'It's hard to forget.' Karen paused, drawn to the older woman with the sweet smile but pained eyes. Impossible to forget. 'Are you from the city?'

She nodded. 'My sister and her husband have been living out here for over thirty years – I come out for a lot of weekends. It's my escape from the city.' She seemed in some inner debate. 'My niece – she was twenty-one – was in the World Trade Center when the planes slammed into the Twin Towers. Nita's been working down there for five months – she was so excited about her job. She's missing . . .'

'I was to be married tomorrow – here on the beach.' Karen fought for composure. 'Greg's among the missing, too.'

Together – compulsively – they talked about the horror that had punctured their lives. Even out here the horror was felt, Karen realized. All over the world, she thought with fresh comprehension. People from so many countries had gone down with the towers. The world grieved.

Caught up in recall of other weekend mornings in Montauk, Karen found her way to the picturesque little restaurant called Bird on the Roof. But arriving there, she hesitated for a moment – assaulted by visions of earlier visits here. Yet, perversely, she felt drawn inside. Here with Greg – with Michelle and Frank – she'd shared such happy times.

She walked inside, somehow relieved that the patronage was light this early in the morning. The staff so friendly – yet even here she felt an undercurrent of pain and shock at what had befallen the country.

She was seated at a tiny table for two along one wall. Just across from the round table she'd shared just two weeks ago. A couple with a pair of little girls – about seven and nine, she judged – were being seated at that table now.

She managed a smile for the friendly waiter who came forward to fill her mug with fresh brewed coffee, ordered the French toast she'd ordered on earlier occasions. The couple at the next table were engaged in an intense conversation. The two small girls were giggling over a Harry Potter book – oblivious to their parents.

'I know what you said,' the youngish woman told the man who sat across from her. 'We're out here to forget

Tuesday's horror. But I can't forget – not when Elaine and Joyce saw all that horror from their classrooms!'

'Hey, they're okay,' he soothed.

'They're having nightmares,' she reproached and sighed. 'So am I.'

'It's crazy to move out here full time . . .' Yet despite his words he seemed ambivalent.

'We love the house out here – we love living in Montauk. I can work from here,' she insisted. 'It won't be easy, I know – but you can work a day or two each week from out here, commute the other days. I don't want to live in the sight of that – that horror. I don't want to worry about the kids every minute they're out of my sight. It won't be forever,' she pushed. 'But until we know we don't have to be afraid every moment of the night – until those lunatics have been dug out of their caves and made to understand they can't remake the world in their image.'

'We'll talk about it tonight,' he hedged, but Karen saw the relief in the woman's eyes. She knew she'd won.

A waitress appeared at their table. Now the focus was on what to order. It was though September 11th had never happened. At least for now.

Karen ate quickly, rejected a second mug of coffee. Walking again on the beach – where early risers were beginning to appear – she dwelt on the heated conversation she'd overheard. She wasn't afraid of more attacks on Manhattan, she analyzed. But she'd have no job, no apartment.

I can't go back to the company with Greg gone – Michelle, Frank, so many others. I couldn't go through that. I can't afford the insane Manhattan rents . . . Can I go back home after all these years?

All at once she felt an urgent need to return to earlier days, to familiar scenes. Even then she'd been a loner – except for a childhood friend through middle school and into high school. Whatever happened to Lisa Cohen? They'd lost track of each other after high school.

She hadn't been home since shortly after her mother died. There'd seemed to be no reason to go back. After college graduation she'd gone on to New York to try to build a new life for herself. To almost ten years of total frustration – until Greg came along.

I'll go back home. She clutched at this decision as though a lifeline to safety. Back home, life moved at a more leisurely pace. She'd find a job of some kind. The cost of living was less than in the city – she wouldn't need a big salary to survive.

The ghosts of that last year of college had been put to rest. Doug didn't return home for the spring holidays. She'd heard that his parents said he was settling somewhere down South. Nor would it have mattered if he had returned, she thought defiantly.

On Monday she would head upstate. Dad would have been pleased, she thought involuntarily. He always said that Weston, New York was the best place in the world.

Six

Karen locked up the Montauk house with an unexpected feeling of trepidation. She must leave here and start a new life for herself. She settled herself in the car, sat gazing into space. She'd turned off the hot water, checked that all the sliders were locked, locked the front door. *All right, head for Weston.*

Traffic was heavy. She fretted at the delays. She'd girded herself for a long haul, but the drive upstate seemed endless. She was conscious of the display of American flags that seemed to say, 'You can't break the spirit of this country.' Again, she reminded herself that the attack on the World Trade Center had not been just an attack on Manhattan. It was an attack on the nation.

She felt a fresh surge of rage at those monsters from the Middle East who had attacked in such hate. How were we to combat fanatics who gloried in dying?

At long last, within a few miles of Weston, Karen's mind darted back through the years. Her growing-up years in Weston had not been happy ones. But then how many people – outside of fiction – enjoyed happy childhoods? Dad used to say that happiness came in small snatches – to be cherished.

The happy times had been those weekends when Dad took her fishing with him. There'd been good times with Lisa Cohen, too, she acknowledged. She and Lisa had been kindred spirits, she thought in tender recall. Both on the outside looking in.

In a small town like Weston – especially all those years ago – most people looked down on Lisa and her parents. They weren't comfortable with bi-racial marriages. Lisa's mother was African-American – though in those days she was called black. Lisa's father – a lawyer – was Jewish. When Lisa was seven he was murdered by a pair of illiterate bigots.

'Karen, you have a way of collecting strange friends,' her mother had commented with an air of distaste when she'd wheedled permission to sleep over at Lisa's house. She secretly pretended that Lisa's mother was hers. Her mother never allowed sleepovers. Her mother didn't laugh a lot. Her mother thought the whole world was against her.

She'd always been at the head of her class, Karen remembered – which had won her the title of teacher's pet through elementary school. In high school the younger sister of a classmate whom she'd beat at a townwide competition had warned her: 'Smart people are never happy.'

She had never thought anything about getting good grades – school had been an escape for her. She'd never looked forward to vacation days. That meant being at home and listening to Mom's litany of minuscule complaints.

Now she was conscious of panic closing in. Was she making a terrible mistake in trying to go home again?

Karen swung off the highway on to the road that would take her into Weston. As she approached a motel a few miles down, she debated about checking in. No, go to a hotel right in town. First thing in the morning she should start looking for a furnished apartment. That wouldn't be a problem here. Would it?

Her heart began to pound as she recognized country roads. But here was a new suburb – where once had been farmland. She drove past attractive homes on large, well-landscaped plots. American flags on display at regular intervals – in recognition that the country was at war. She realized, too, that Weston had grown in her absence.

Now she was arriving in familiar territory. Who was living in their house? She vaguely remembered the out-of-town couple who had bought it. They had three kids, were anxious about the quality of the school system.

How many of those with whom she'd gone to school still lived here? These days families were so scattered. And then she tensed at the sight of a gray ranch with yellow shutters that sat on a corner plot close to town. The house where Doug had lived when they were both in high school. Just two blocks from her own house.

Doug hadn't returned to his family at the end of the school year. There had been rumors that he was married – but then she'd known that. Another reason for her wanting to leave Weston after her mother died was not to have to face the gray ranch with yellow shutters. Did Doug's parents still live there?

She had known him in their high-school days – they'd even been in the same classes at times. She remembered that he'd once made a tentative move towards asking her out. But she'd been so insecure – so fearful – that she'd brushed him off. Why would such a popular boy want to date her?

It wasn't until their senior year at college that they'd become more than casual classmates. In truth, she'd rarely seen him until that last year – when again they'd shared a class. He'd been so sympathetic about her parents' death. So quickly they'd become involved.

But don't think about that painful break-up. Even now she felt sick in recall. Bless Greg for bringing her out of that. But now Greg was gone. No more men in her life, she warned herself yet again. She'd struck out twice. There'd be no third.

Driving into town – traffic light on this Monday afternoon, flags on display everywhere – she was immediately conscious of changes. Here was an aura of decay. At intervals stores were boarded up, slapped with out-of-date political posters. Shopfronts cried out for paint, repairs.

She saw a pair of men laboriously scrubbing windows of a modest grocery store. She was startled when she realized they were trying to wash away graffiti. Anti-Arab graffiti. An Arab problem here in Weston? It was a disconcerting thought.

Now the anguish that had enveloped her like a second skin was being penetrated by a simmering rage. How could a lunatic fringe turn the world upside-down this way? In a sudden need for confirmation of this new rage she reached to turn on the car radio.

A newscaster spewed forth an array of shocking statistics. The deaths at the World Trade Center continued to be estimated in the thousands. More than were killed at Pearl Harbor, she taunted herself. In a matter of minutes innocent men, women and children had been murdered.

Weston was a world removed from Manhattan. A safe small town – where every unexpected sound wouldn't terrify her. She wouldn't look out her apartment window to see the smoldering ruins of the World Trade Center. But she couldn't blot out of her mind the signs of anti-Arab graffiti on that store window. Arabs here in Weston? Friendly Arabs – or secret followers of Osama bin Laden?

Driving on she discovered that segments of Main Street exuded an atmosphere of prosperity. But long-time favorite local shops were gone. The specialty shop where she'd bought school clothes every fall. The shoe store where her first pair of shoes had been bought, and shoes through her growing-up years. Her high-school hangout for burgers and shakes.

The ubiquitous chains had moved in. McDonald's, the Gap, P.C. Richards, Pizza Hut. Her eyes swept over the line-up. Was every town in America doomed to be a carbon copy of the others?

She was oddly relieved when she saw the old Weston Court Hotel still in existence. It had been renovated since she last saw it. And she suspected the rates had shot upward through the years. She slowed down to a crawl, noted that parking space for hotel guests was at the rear.

In the parking area she removed her weekender, hesitated about the safety of the loaded trunk and rear of the car. No problem, she chided herself – this wasn't New York. She locked the car and headed into the hotel via the rear entrance.

The Weston Court – like part of the town – had undergone lavish refurbishing. The nightly rents would no doubt reflect this, Karen assumed – conscious of her limited funds. She crossed the carpeted, elegantly furnished lobby to the registration desk.

Waiting for the clerk to complete a phone call, she scanned the headline of *The Star*, which lay across the desk. 'ARAB-AMERICAN CONSTRUCTION WORKER BEATEN.' All at once she was ice cold. She'd thought – naively – that here in Weston she could run away from the ugliness that was stifling Manhattan.

The Star, she recalled, had long been regarded as an ultra-conservative newspaper. It had pushed its competition out of business a dozen years ago. Some things remained unchanged in Weston.

The registration clerk came to her with an apologetic smile. In moments she had registered and was being escorted to her room. She was conscious of gratitude that the hotel rose only six stories high. Would there ever be a time again when she could walk into a skyscraper without fear?

Alone in her fifth-floor room, she crossed to the expanse of windows to flip on the air-conditioner. She hesitated a moment, then opened the drapes. Her room looked down on a small, lovely courtyard, where colorful coleus and early chrysanthemums bloomed.

She lifted her valise on to the queen-size bed. Did everybody sleep on queen-sized beds these days? She unpacked, needing activity, then realized she was hungry. A rare event on these last traumatic days. Go downstairs, find a café, she told herself. Long ago she'd learned the exorbitant prices in hotel restaurants.

In the humid afternoon she walked along unfamiliar Main Street until she approached a café that had been here ever since she could remember. A family café, she recalled – where on occasional weekend mornings she had gone with Dad for coffee before a day of fishing.

She walked into the lightly populated café, grateful for the air-conditioning on the humid day, crossed to a corner booth for two. An amiable waitress crossed to take her order. She settled for a sliced turkey sandwich and coffee.

Two burly men in chinos and tee shirts straddled stools at the counter and talked in over-loud tones that drowned out the low-keyed radio.

'Hey, he probably asked for it. You know them immigrants,' one drawled. 'They think they own the world. How come we got Arabs livin' here, anyway? Who needs 'em?'

'Look what they did down in New York. We don't want that happenin' here,' the other said. 'A good Arab is a dead Arab.'

The waiter behind the counter appeared uncomfortable, exchanged a loaded glance with the pair of waitresses on duty. *How awful to talk like that! To think that way! But if I see someone who appears as though he's from the Middle East, I'm terrified. I shouldn't feel that way – but I do.*

'Let 'em all go down to New York,' the other man at the counter said with a raucous laugh. 'Or send them back where they came from.'

'My old lady is pissed about us havin' to run down to New York tomorrow. She don't like us goin' through the tunnel.'

'So we'll take the bridge.' The other shrugged this off. 'Whichever way we're gonna waste a lot of time with all them inspections they got goin' now.'

'Bridge, tunnel – they both scare the hell out of Mame. She says I don't carry no life insurance. I'm worth more to her alive than dead.' His guffaw was enough to crack a window, Karen thought in distaste, and was relieved when the two men made a hasty departure at the appearance of a fellow worker at the door.

Karen ate without tasting. She'd come here, running away from the memory of the morning of September 11th. But here she sensed the same fear. Would she ever be able to gaze at a turbaned man or a woman with the traditional Arab headscarf and not feel afraid?

Have I made a mistake in coming home? But where else is there for me to go?

Seven

Karen headed back for the hotel, paused at a news-stand to pick up a copy of *The Star*. Start looking at the listings of furnished apartments, she exhorted herself – and the Help Wanted. The cost of her hotel room was unnerving. And first thing in the morning open a checking account.

She returned to her room, settled down to study the classified ads – ignoring the headline story. But the conversation she'd heard in the café haunted her. It was wrong of those men to feel such rage – yet in a lopsided way she understood. These were harrowing times.

There was a minuscule listing of furnished apartments. Later she'd buy furniture – when she was working, with a steady salary coming in. For now it would have to be a furnished apartment. She checked off two listings of meager promise. She glanced at her watch. Too late to call now. As for jobs, she couldn't afford to be selective, she warned herself.

All at once she felt herself drained of strength. She'd slept little last night – or any night since Tuesday. OK, stretch out on the bed, watch TV. She flipped on the television set, found a news program, and moments later switched it off. She couldn't face more ghastly statistics. She couldn't watch replays of the burning infernos that had been the Twin Towers.

The night ahead seemed an endless swathe of time. Once this had been home – all she knew. Now she felt herself an alien on a strange planet. What had happened through the years to Lisa Cohen? Lisa had vowed to get away, live in a big city. '*Half the people in this town resent me because I'm black. The other half resent me because I'm Jewish. I don't fit the acceptable mold.*'

She'd loved Lisa's mother. Rachel Cohen was bright, articulate, and unflappable. She'd taught in a junior high school and had earned respect from students who initially looked down upon her because of the color of her skin.

'We might as well be living in the Deep South of thirty years ago,' Rae Cohen once remarked, knowing that *she* – even in her teens – would understand.

She hadn't seen Lisa or her mother since a few days after high school graduation. They'd moved to a town seventy miles away. She and Lisa had vowed to keep in touch – but when they'd gone away to college in different states, Lisa to a predominately black school in the South, they'd lost touch.

Where is Lisa now? She might have been in New York in those years when I was there. We might have lived on the same street. Why did we let ourselves lose touch?

On impulse she leaned over to the night table, reached for the local phone book. It was ridiculous to think Lisa might be living here now. She flipped through the pages and stared in disbelief. There she was: Lisa Cohen, 215 Elm Street. Not the house where she'd lived all those years ago.

For the first time since she'd said good-bye to Greg on Tuesday morning, Karen felt a surge of pleasure. Lisa was here. Not everything in the world had changed.

She punched in Lisa's phone number, waiting with pounding heart. It couldn't be another Lisa Cohen, she rejected. Could it?

'Hello.' Ten years later she still recognized Lisa's voice.

'Lisa, it's me – Karen. Karen Hunter.'

'Karen!' Her voice blended astonishment, delight, tenderness. 'Are you here in Weston?'

'I just arrived this afternoon.' Karen took a deep breath. 'I was down in New York. After what happened I had to get away . . .'

'Oh, God – it must have been awful.'

'I can't believe something so horrible could happen in this country.' Karen struggled for composure.

'I have a brief session coming up in a moment with a client – I'm a social worker,' Lisa explained. 'But what about dinner? Could you meet me around six thirty? I'm dying to see you!'

'Sure thing. Where?'

'There's a great Italian restaurant at the edge of town. Antonio's. You always liked Italian,' Lisa recalled.

'Especially your mom's Italian.' Her own mother had been an uninspired, reluctant cook. 'How do I get there? I have a car,' Karen added. In New York it was not an essential item.

Lisa gave her directions, said she'd reserve a table. Karen felt a surge of relief that in little over an hour she'd be sitting down to dinner with her childhood best friend.

'There's my doorbell,' Lisa said hurriedly. 'See you at six thirty.'

A few minutes ahead of schedule Karen sat at a table in a private corner of Antonio's. Only a few tables occupied at this hour, but she suspected it would be fully occupied later. She assumed Lisa was single – or was she divorced? Her mind was bursting with questions. The memories of all those years ago had rushed back into her consciousness.

The room exuded friendliness, she thought as she glanced around at the white stuccoed walls, hung with colorful portraits of Italian landmarks. Though it was early, already a waiter was moving about the tables to light the squat, red candles.

Then she saw Lisa's tall, lithe figure striding towards her. Lisa wore the years well, Karen decided. There was an aura of confidence about her that had been painfully missing all those years ago – when she'd sometimes declared she belonged nowhere. Not black – not white.

Lisa's mother – whom she was allowed, with much pride, to call Rae – declared that Lisa had the best of both worlds. Still – in Weston – her mother had brought her up to consider herself black. '*Because you won't ever be accepted as white*,' Rae had repeated at intervals – realistic, without rancor. '*That's the way the world operates.*'

Karen rose from her chair, took a step forward to embrace Lisa.

'Oh, honey, it's so good to see you!' Lisa crooned, then stepped back for a better look. 'I always knew you'd grow into a beauty.'

'Always the flatterer.' Karen sat down again with a sense of well-being she hadn't felt since early morning of September 11th.

'Oh, there's so much I want to know . . .' Lisa searched Karen's face. 'It's been rough,' she surmised after a moment.

Haltingly, Karen told her about meeting Greg, about how he'd changed her life – and then about the morning five days before they were to be married.

'I didn't know where to go.' Karen forced a shaky smile. 'I know the old cliché – "you can't go home again." But here I am.'

'You did right,' Lisa encouraged.

Their waiter arrived. For a few moments they focused on ordering. Karen impressed by the low prices in local restaurants – in such contrast to New York. Then their waiter hurried off to the kitchen.

'Now, tell me about you,' Karen ordered.

'I went to that college down south that we talked about our last year in high school. But I didn't quite belong there. I transferred to NYU – and that was cool.'

'You were in New York,' Karen said with amazement. 'And I never knew.'

'I earned my masters in social work at Columbia – six months before Mom died. Thank God, she lived to see me graduate. She'd worked so hard for that.'

'Oh, Lisa—' Fresh pain poured over Karen. Rae had been a wonderful woman. Why did the good so often die young? And she remembered again how so many of the faces of the 'missing' that lined storefronts, lamp posts and walls in Manhattan had been young.

'I'm so glad you came back,' Lisa said tenderly.

'How do you like your work?' Karen pursued.

'It's tiring and so often frustrating – but I wouldn't want to do anything else.' Lisa hesitated. 'Right now it's rough. After what happened at the World Trade Center . . .'

'Why rough up here?' Karen's eyes were questioning. 'Oh, you mean people up here lost loved ones down there.'

'That, too.' Lisa nodded. 'But we have a small group of people from the Middle East – families that have been here for years. One family came, found it good – and others followed. The second generations were born here. There's one family that arrived here in 1897. But yesterday a young Arab-American – he'd earned his BA from State and was working on a construction job to earn money for architectural school – was beaten so badly because he's of Arab descent that he's been hospitalized.'

'I saw the headline in *The Star*,' Karen recalled. And remembered the conversation between the two truck drivers in the café. 'It's awful, Lisa – but people have been so hurt.' *I hurt – for Greg, for Michelle and Frank, for all the others in the company who couldn't escape.*

'That's no reason to make innocent people suffer because they happen to have been born in Arab nations – or with parents who were born there,' Lisa objected.

'I realize that,' Karen said defensively. *But in my heart I'm afraid. How do I root out this fear? Will it be with me forever? I feel so guilty.*

'You'll be looking for an apartment,' Lisa surmised, deliberately switching topics, and Karen was grateful.

'Right.' Karen sighed. 'I looked in *The Star*. The pickings seem slim.'

Lisa hesitated. 'I'd suggest you move in with me until you find a place.' Her voice apologetic now. 'But I have a friend – male – who has visiting privileges.' She hesitated. 'Howie would like to make it a permanent arrangement – like marriage – but I'm not ready for that. We both have crazy hours. He's a pediatrician – white and Jewish.'

'Like your father,' Karen reminded her.

'His parents slaved to put him through medical school. They don't know about me. I don't think I'm their version of the perfect daughter-in-law.'

'You'd be marrying Howie – not his parents.' But Karen understood her reluctance.

'I know Howie wants a family – but I won't have children to live in this world. Knowing how rough life could be for them. But enough about me.' Lisa brushed this aside. 'You need an apartment.'

'I'll find something,' Karen said with shaky optimism.

'I know of a tiny furnished apartment that's for rent. Actually it's illegal – being in a one-family zone. But everybody looks the other way.' Lisa chuckled. 'Everybody in this town either loves Amy Lansing – or fears her. She's eighty-three, looks like sixty-three, and thinks like thirty-three. She's opinionated, says what she thinks, and is determined to make this a better town.'

'I remember her.' Karen nodded in recall. 'When we helped out one summer at the Senior Citizens Center, she was there – as a volunteer.' That was seventeen years ago – but all at once it seemed yesterday. Karen clutched at this touch with the past – when life had been less complicated.

Lisa chuckled. 'She's still volunteering. Some people claim she asks for exorbitant rent – but she's fighting for survival. Her husband died nine years ago – and there went one Social Security check. I understand the house is hers free and clear, but property taxes keep going up and there're the usual repairs.'

'Should I call her and ask if the apartment's still available?'

'I'll call her right now.' Lisa reached in her purse for her cell phone, punched in a number.

Moments later, Lisa was off the phone. 'The apartment is still available. We'll run over for a look after dinner.'

'Great.' Karen felt a surge of relief. One major problem might be solved. 'The town's grown since I left – but basically it seems the same.' She wanted to believe it was the same.

'There've been changes.' Lisa's face tightened. 'It started eight years ago – when Hank Fredericks was elected mayor. He had *The Star* behind him – and a lot of money.' She grimaced in recall. 'And he made great promises. None of which he kept.'

'But he gets re-elected?'

'You got it. But now there're a lot of disgruntled voters. He's as corrupt as they come, only concerned with big payoffs.' Lisa held up crossed fingers. 'With a little luck we'll elect Tony Mendoza. Still, Mendoza has a tough fight these next few weeks.'

'Why?' Karen probed.

'He was born in Mexico. It doesn't matter that he's lived here in Weston since he was three . . .'

'I don't think I remember him.' Karen squinted in thought. But then she'd never been involved in local politics.

'The family never moved in our circles.' Lisa's smile was wry. 'His parents ran a mom-and-pop grocery store in the low-income part of town. They worked hard, put their three kids through college. Tony became a lawyer. His sister teaches at the elementary school. The brother sells insurance. Tony has been fighting local corruption ever since

Fredericks showed his hand. I'm a volunteer in his campaign.'

Karen thought about her prospective landlady – still volunteering at eighty-three. 'I'll bet Mrs Lansing is one of his volunteers.'

'Call her Amy,' Lisa said. 'Everybody does.'

Amy Lansing's house – built in the early 1900s – was in an older section of town that had seen more affluent days. An ornate, white-shingled, two-storey structure with a porch that extended on three sides. A paint job would be needed soon, Karen thought – sympathetic to Amy's budget.

The small plot was meticulously maintained. The windows shone – an American flag displayed in one window. There was something oddly reassuring about Amy Lansing's house, Karen decided as Lisa pulled into the driveway.

The door opened as Karen and Lisa approached. A small woman with delicate features and short white hair – appearing elegant even in casual slacks and turtleneck top – smiled in welcome.

'I like people who're punctual.' Amy Lansing greeted them in approval, waiting for a formal introduction. She inspected Karen. 'I remember you,' she declared. 'Your father was my accountant for almost twenty years. He's been missed in this town. Now we have a bunch of smart-alecky kids working at that chain deal – don't know their ass from a hole in the ground. But they're cheap and people flock there.'

'Not everybody,' Lisa pointed out good-humoredly. 'We still have a few bona fide CPAs in town.'

'But enough chit-chat. Let me show you the apartment.' Amy hesitated. 'I always admired your father. He was a good man. In his quiet way he did a lot for this town. For Cliff Hunter's daughter,' she added in a conspiratorial whisper, 'the rent drops twenty per cent.'

'Thank you.' *Maybe I can fit in here. Maybe in this town*

– so far from that horror in Manhattan – I'll be able to sleep again.

Amy Lansing led them to the apartment she'd fashioned from a segment of the first floor of the house. A small living room, smaller bedroom, and a closet of a kitchen. The furniture spoke of an earlier time, but there was an air of serenity here. *Yes, I can live here.*

In a matter of minutes the deal was closed. She'd move into the apartment in the morning. Amy – as she insisted Karen call her – gave her instructions about rushing through telephone and cable TV services.

'Go over first thing in the morning,' Amy told her. 'Tell the girls on duty you're my guest.' She chuckled. 'That's playing the game – I'm not supposed to have a tenant. They'll have workmen over here the same day.'

'I will,' Karen promised. On sight she'd felt that Amy was one of those rare people on her own wavelength. Thank God she'd called Lisa.

'If you're like me,' Amy confided, 'I can't live without my cable TV. I'm a news junkie.' Her face was pained. 'But I suspect for now you'd just as soon avoid the news?' Her smile was warm and sympathetic.

'That's right.' Karen's own smile was wan.

Karen and Lisa left the house, headed for the car. Karen glanced up at the star-splashed sky. As in Montauk, Karen stared in wonder. In the city it was so rare to be aware of stars in the sky, the lovely light of the moon.

'It's a beautiful night,' Lisa said and Karen nodded in agreement.

And then she froze in shock and disbelief. Her eyes fastened to a man emerging from a house across the way. Her mind was playing tricks on her, she told herself.

That can't be Doug walking down the path of that house. He moved away from town our last year in college. But it is Doug.

Eight

Doug slid behind the wheel of his car, sat immobile, and stared into the night without seeing. His heart was pounding, his mouth suddenly dry. He was mistaken – surely that wasn't Karen walking out of the house across the way. It was someone who resembled Karen.

I haven't seen her in almost ten years. She must have changed. That's someone who resembles her – the way she looked all those years ago. I'm hallucinating.

When he returned to Weston two years ago, he'd been so impatient to see her. Hoping to try to explain the insanity of those last days before he left college. Even now he felt sick in recall.

His mind shot back through the years, to the evening that reshaped his life. Just a few evenings before he began to see Karen . . .

Doug sprawled in a chair in the tiny living room of the off-campus apartment he shared with Jason and Bill. He was trying to focus on cramming for an exam on Monday. Then Jason popped in, insisted he go to a bash at a nearby sorority house.

'Man, you've got the whole weekend to cram. Friday night's for partying. Don't be a nerd.'

'I can't afford to let my grades slide down – not with law school breathing down my neck.' But part of him yearned for a break from the school grind.

'One night?' Jason jeered. 'Dump the books. Let's go!'
Doug hesitated a moment. 'Okay, cool it. We'll go.'

But he couldn't entirely dismiss a feeling of guilt. He
knew it was a sacrifice for his parents to deal with law
school costs – even if he worked after the first year.
Everybody said the first year of law school was a bitch –
Dad and Mom insisted he was to focus on studies that first
year. They were refinancing the mortgage on the house to
cover law-school costs.

By the time he and Jason arrived, the bash was in full
swing. Right through school he'd steered clear of any lasting
relationship. He knew he wanted to be a lawyer. He knew
what a grind law-school would be – and the hardships it would
cost his parents financially. College was no time to play.

'Hey, look at that sexy dish across the room,' Jason whispered. 'She's stripping you down to your skin.' He whistled eloquently. 'Wow, she's a hot one.'

She was walking – slinking was the word that popped
into his mind – in his direction. She wore one of those
eight-inch skirts below a tight-fitting sweater cut down as
far as the law allowed without her being arrested for in-
decent exposure.

'Hi,' she drawled, leaning forward so that he had a star-
tling view down the v-neck of her sweater. 'I'm Candy.
Who're you?'

'Doug.' He cleared his throat, aware of arousal. Jason
and Bill had nicknamed him 'the monk' two years ago. He
didn't feel like a monk right now.

'I've been waiting the whole school year for some guy
who really turns me on,' she said lustily. 'I'm tired of being
a virgin. It's so boring.' She giggled as she draped her arms
about him and thrust her hips against his.

There'd been just that one night with Candy. He'd drunk
too much – but not too much to perform. Then she disappeared from his life. He hadn't seen her again until almost

four months later – when he and Karen were planning the rest of their lives together. Candy had buzzed and said she had to see him. It was important.

'You have to meet me, Doug,' she insisted, sounding on the verge of hysteria. 'If you don't I'll – I'll do something desperate.'

Reluctant, but with no inkling of what awaited him – that his whole life was about to be turned upside down – he'd gone to meet her at a coffee hangout at the edge of town.

They carried their espresso to a corner table that provided some privacy. He tried to figure out why she'd been so insistent on meeting him. Remembering their night together, he was nervous. But hell, that was four months ago.

He hadn't seen her since that night, he told himself. They'd just had a one-night stand. He'd made no effort to call. She hadn't called him. It had just been having too many beers, he'd told himself. And she was experimenting. He remembered her sultry voice: '*I'm tired of being a virgin. It's so boring.*'

Ignoring her espresso, she leaned forward and said quietly, 'Doug, I'm pregnant.'

'Candy, we – we were together four months ago.' He gaped in disbelief. *What was she trying to pull?* But he was suddenly aware that she had abandoned her eight-inch skirt, the tight-as-skin sweater. She wore a loose shirt that hung over baggy slacks.

'I'm four months pregnant. At first I thought I was just late – then I knew. I'm Catholic, Doug.'

Jason and Bill told him he was crazy. Women went to abortion clinics – they didn't carry through unwanted pregnancies. They scoffed at his admission that she'd been a virgin when they slept together. '*God, Doug, you're so damn naive. Women fake. They think it excites a guy to believe he got there first.*'

But he'd been raised to recognize responsibilities, to do

the right thing. He couldn't walk away from this. He loved Karen with an intensity he'd never believed possible. He knew he wanted to spend the rest of his life with her. But he couldn't do that now.

He called Karen – he couldn't face her in person. He told her he was leaving school. That something happened – and he was getting married. It had been cold and brutal – but he hadn't known any other way to do it.

Mom and Dad had been upset – they saw him through the final year of college in another state and then law school. They couldn't understand what was happening. He'd been kind of preparing them for Karen – knowing that they'd be upset at his marrying so young. Then he told them about Candy.

Had he seen Karen a few minutes ago? Could he have another chance at a whole life? Could he make her understand?

Relieved that Lisa was in a rush to return to her apartment, Karen drove back to her hotel, hurried upstairs to her room. She sought out the local phone directory. Fingers trembling, she flipped the pages until she found the listings beginning with 'M'. Her eyes sped down the list of names.

Here it was: Douglas Madison. A residential address and number and the same for his office. He'd gone to law school. He was a practicing attorney.

She moved about her room in a daze, prepared for bed. But she couldn't blot from her mind the realization that Doug had returned to Weston in the years she'd been away.

Those ghastly last weeks at school seemed like yesterday. She closed her eyes and heard Doug – abject, fighting to speak to her on the phone. '*Karen, I'm so sorry. Something's happened. I have to leave school. I–I'm getting married.*' He'd hung up and disappeared from her life.

She recalled the weird rumors floating about – none of which made sense. Only Jason had been honest. '*Doug knocked up some student on campus. They left school. They're getting married.'*

How could she stay here when there was every likelihood she'd encounter Doug one day? She flinched at the vision of walking down the street and coming face to face with Doug – with his wife and his child. The anguish of all those years ago suffused her again.

She'd felt so stupid, so naive – to have believed Doug when he said they'd marry after graduation, be together forever. He'd go to law school. She'd study for a masters in journalism. It was to be a whole new world for her. And then she'd crashed to earth. All the old fears, inhibitions, had taken her prisoner. Only for a little while – with Greg – she had felt a whole person again.

I wasn't imagining it. That was Doug coming out of the house across from my new apartment. How can I stay here?

Nine

With a subconscious reluctance to face the new day, Karen crept into wakefulness. Now the trauma she'd felt at seeing Doug returned. How could she endure living in this town, never knowing when she'd run into Doug? How could she feel this way after all these years? She'd thought that period of her life was buried forever.

I must stop running. There has to be a place where I can pull my life together – but where? No way can I face living in New York – even if the company returns to operation and offered me a job. It would be re-living a nightmare.

Talk to Lisa, she ordered herself. She had found a new, strong Lisa last night. Again she was trying to cling to someone, she scolded herself. When would she learn to stand on her own two feet? For a little while there had been Doug – and then the awful barren years until Greg came into her life.

Lisa has learned to control her life. It's time for me to do the same.

In a sudden need for action, she thrust aside the sheet and strode into the bathroom. She'd shower, dress, call Lisa and ask if they could meet for breakfast. Let Lisa help her decide if she could handle living in the same town with Doug and his family.

Standing under the brisk hot shower, she tried to frame words to explain her situation to Lisa. Oh, this was crazy.

She was 31 years old. Other women her age were married, had families, held down responsible positions.

But she was so tired, so afraid of tomorrow – and at the back of her mind she knew this was a monumental turning point in her life. *Talk to Lisa. This is what she does for a living – and she's my only true friend.*

Dressed for the day – which should have included job hunting – her mind exhorted, she sat at the edge of the bed and reached for the phone. She hesitated. Was it too early to call Lisa? Call, she decided. Later, Lisa might have left for work.

'Hello.' Lisa's voice was warm. Karen remembered Lisa said that clients called her at often insane hours with their tormenting problems.

'Lisa, it's me.' Karen struggled to sound casual. 'I was wondering if you'd be able to have breakfast with me this morning. I–I have a problem. I need feedback from you.'

'Of course, Karen.' Now Lisa was serious – as though she understood the effort this call for help had cost. 'Let's meet in about fifteen minutes at the Main Street Diner.' Lisa's voice softened. 'It's still there at the same place. Remember how we used to feel so grown up when we'd run there for lunch instead of eating at the high-school cafeteria?'

'Oh, I remember.' Nostalgia soared in Karen. They were the two loners always striving to appear sophisticated. 'In fifteen minutes, Lisa.'

Karen drove into town – reminding herself that after breakfast she must go to the telephone company and to the cable company to arrange for service. If Lisa could persuade her to remain in Weston. Her mind was in such turmoil.

Walking into the diner she felt time zooming backwards. Little had changed here in the 16 years since she and Lisa had played their little game of dashing here for lunch – as though they were past high-school age and working at grown-up jobs. The same Utrillo prints hung on the walls

– alternating with mirrored panels. The same simulated red-leather upholstered booths.

With the sense of being an interloper she scanned the occupants of the booth. This was the height of the morning rush. Few booths were empty. No, Lisa hadn't arrived yet. Her eyes lighted on an empty booth at the rear. She hurried down the aisle to claim it.

Moments later Lisa arrived.

'As usual the phone rang when I was already at the door. Don't let anybody ever tell you social workers work from 9 to 5. It's a 24/7 job.'

A waiter came to take their orders. Obviously Lisa was a regular at the diner. They ordered. As the waiter left their booth, Lisa leaned forward with a tender smile.

'You have a problem.'

Haltingly, Karen told Lisa of her affair with Doug all those years ago. Admitting the havoc it had wreaked in her.

'Seeing him last night was – devastating.' She frowned in thought. 'Maybe I was especially vulnerable because of what happened with Greg. There are moments when I just can't believe he's gone, Lisa. Greg was so good to me.'

'I know Doug, of course.' Lisa was somber. 'But I didn't notice him last night.'

'You were admiring Amy Lansing's coleuses,' Karen reminded her. 'I don't know if I can deal with running into him and his wife.' Jason's words about Doug's wife darted across her mind: '*She was an oversexed bitch Doug met at a sorority house party.*'

'Doug's divorced,' Lisa told her. Karen was startled. 'Before their first anniversary, the way I hear it. He went on to finish law school, opened an office here in town. He's active in local politics. People expect him to run for the Town Council some time soon.' Lisa hesitated. 'He's got a stream of singles chasing him, but the word is he won't play.'

'I know it's absurd to be afraid of running into him.' *So*

he was divorced. What did that mean to her? 'What about the child he had with his ex-wife?'

'Nobody in town knows anything about a kid,' Lisa dismissed this. 'Maybe his ex-wife has full custody.' Lisa's eyes searched hers. 'You still feel something for Doug?'

'No,' Karen rejected defiantly. 'I've had it with men.' *Twice, life seemed so beautiful – then the horrific endings.* 'I won't leave myself open to that kind of hurt again. Not ever.'

'Stay here.' Lisa was firm. 'For the most part this is a good town, with good people. You have a comfortable little apartment. You'll find a job here. You'll meet new friends, get involved in local activities. Karen, you remember me back in our school days. We were the two misfits. But I told myself it didn't have to be that way. Other people didn't look on us as being weird – we created so many misconceptions.'

'I'll give it a try.' Karen's smile was shaky. Ambivalent.

Lisa seemed to be in mental debate for a few moments. 'Doug's very well liked. Tony Mendoza admits he would have been afraid to tackle this campaign without Doug behind him. People laugh sometimes and ask if Doug ever takes out time to sleep. He has his law practice – he's always fighting for something good for this town. He's a part-time assistant district attorney. It'll be difficult,' Lisa conceded, 'not to be aware of his presence.'

'I'll have to deal with that.' *I won't let Doug drive me away.*

Again, Lisa appeared to be searching for words. 'We have a situation right now in town,' Lisa plunged in. 'That bright, sweet guy that I told you about – the one in the headlines. His parents fled from Iraq when he was a baby – back in 1980, I think – to escape the violence that broke out when the Islam Republic was formed and Iraq invaded Iran.'

Karen tensed. 'The man who was beat up because he's an Arab,' she recalled. And all once she visualized the horrific scenes being flashed constantly on TV – the huge planes, in the hands of Arabs, slashing into the Twin Towers.

'Marty Mohammed is an Arab-American,' Lisa emphasized. 'He's lived in this country for most of his life.'

'I read the newspaper article.' She couldn't lie to Lisa, ever, Karen told herself. 'The older sister of those two men is missing at the World Trade Center. They were badly shaken.'

'That didn't give them the right to punish an innocent person,' Lisa objected. 'We have a small group of Arab-Americans here in Weston – and they're all scared to death. The women are even afraid to leave their houses to go to shop for food.'

'I'm sure this was an isolated incident.' But now Karen remembered the graffiti she'd seen on the shop window when she was driving into town. So there were two incidents. 'People are terribly upset. This country has never seen such horror before – it's unreal to us.'

'I've just begun to organize a group of women who'll accompany our Arab-American wives and mothers on routine trips like shopping at the mall or at local stores. We have to make them feel safe. We'll work out schedules that fit into our daily lives. Come and join the group.'

Karen flinched. 'I can't,' she said. 'You weren't there – you didn't see what happened at the World Trade Center. You haven't walked along streets lined with photographs of missing people. Sent to their deaths by fanatical Arabs.'

'But these aren't fanatical Arabs,' Lisa began gently. 'They're—'

'We don't know,' Karen broke in. She felt her face grow hot. 'Those men who hijacked those planes and ploughed them into the Twin Towers and the Pentagon – they'd blended right in with Americans. Nobody guessed what they meant to do.'

'Okay,' Lisa soothed. 'So you're still too close to that

horror. Settle yourself into your apartment, start job hunting. You have a resumé,' she assumed. 'I'll make copies for you on the office machine if you don't have them.'

'I haven't even thought about a resumé,' Karen admitted.

'You didn't expect to be job hunting.' Lisa's smile was wry. 'I know – it's been an awful jolt.'

'I was at my last job for almost three years. It was the first time I'd stayed anywhere that long. That's where I met Greg.'

'All right.' Lisa's voice was brisk now. 'Work up your resumé. Explain about your company being situated at the World Trade Center – how they're having to search for new quarters. But you felt the time had arrived to return to your hometown. People will be very sympathetic. You'll land something good. Maybe not in the first few days,' she acknowledged, 'but you'll latch on to something substantial.'

The waiter arrived with their orders. They settled down to eat. In Lisa's mind it was settled, Karen thought. Lisa was convinced she should remain here.

'Karen, Doug's prosecuting those two guys who beat up Marty Mohammed.' *I'm not surprised. Doug was always ready to fight for what he thought was a just cause.* 'I suspect nobody else in the DA's office wanted to take it on. The arraignment's this evening. Sophie Mohammed – Marty's mother – tells me Doug's convinced they'll be held for a grand jury hearing, that they'll go to trial. And that's going to split this town right down the middle.'

'What about the newspapers? Where do they stand?'

'Just where you'd think if you knew them. *The Star* is screaming for an acquittal. *The Sentinel* demands a trial and conviction.' Lisa frowned in frustration for an instant, then tried to brush aside the subject. 'Come over to my apartment for dinner this evening,' Lisa said. 'I'll throw something together. Howie's at a convention in San Francisco this week,' she explained. 'I'm as free as a bird.'

'Did he fly out there?' Karen asked involuntarily, brushed by alarm. 'I mean—' she hesitated, gestured ineffectually.

'Yeah, I was scared till he called from there. And I'll be scared when it's time for his return flight. But we can't go through life terrified all the time. The country's forewarned now – we can fly without visions of disaster. At least, that's what I tell myself,' Lisa confessed.

'Driving up here I was terrified at having to cross first the Throggs Neck Bridge and then the Tappen Zee.' Karen shivered in recall.

'I spoke with Marty's mother this morning. The fellow who was beat up,' Lisa said in answer to Karen's blank stare. 'I've known her ever since she and her two sons moved here nine years ago. She's a fine, intelligent woman. She opened a small gift shop, built it up into a successful venture. Before she came here, her husband had gone back to Iraq to try to bring his sister and her husband out. The three of them died in an Iraqi prison.'

'I'll unload the car at the apartment.' Karen derailed the conversation. *I didn't expect to encounter problems here in Weston. Why am I so fearful after September 11th?* 'But first I'll run over to take care of phone service and cable. I'll pick up *The Star* and read the Help Wanted column.' *Why am I running on like this?* 'I don't remember *The Sentinel . . .*'

'No. *The Sentinel* began operation about seven years ago. You know what this town used to be like,' Lisa reminded Karen. 'Solid Republican. But that's changing – and *The Sentinel* has picked up a small but growing following.'

'I'll check the job listings in both newspapers,' Karen promised, planning to focus on finding a job. With no income, her cash reserve would soon ebb away. 'I'll work on my resumé and bring it over at dinner.'

How can I talk this way? As though the world we've always known still exists. So I'm three hours north of New York City – I can look out my windows without seeing the empty space where the Twin Towers once stood. But will I ever forget that Greg and Michelle and Frank – and thousands of other people – lie buried beneath a hundred plus floors of rubble?

Will I ever sleep through the night without enduring tormenting nightmares?

Ten

Doug sat at Marty's hospital bedside and assured him – with synthetic conviction – that the two men who'd attacked him would be punished. He was apprehensive about the reaction of a local jury, still shaken by the events of September 11th.

'Why did they do this to me?' Marty demanded for the dozenth time. 'What did I ever do to hurt them?' He paused. His eyes rebellious. 'I know I'm an Arab.'

'You're an Arab-American,' Doug corrected, emphasizing American.

'I worry about my mom. I worry about my brother. Why did he have to start growing a beard?' Marty slammed a fist on the table beside his bed in frustration. 'He came home furious from his job two nights ago. He said one of the guys called him Joseph bin Laden!'

'We have a few hotheads in town. But they'll cool off.' *Will they, considering the current climate?* 'Once they see the two creeps who punched you around sentenced to jail terms.'

'You expect Cal and Bart Henderson to be convicted?' Marty was derisive. 'After what's happened at the World Trade Center and the Pentagon? And my stupid brother is telling my mother she should not be walking out in public without her hair covered! I came here as a baby. He was born in this country! Why is he trying to change things now?'

65

'If your mother wants to observe orthodox Muslim law, she has the right to do that. Just as your brother has the right to grow a beard.' Unexpectedly Doug chuckled. 'I was the only student ever to start my high school wearing a beard. I'd been on a school trip to Spain the previous summer. For a lark I'd run a razor over my face – and the beard followed. But nobody denied me the right to wear a beard.'

'They're letting me out of here tomorrow morning,' Marty said, churning with impatience. 'I can't go back to work for a few days. I hate losing the money – I'll need every cent I can make in the next eleven months to get into architectural school next September.' He hesitated. 'Why are people linking everybody with Arab blood into one category? Most of us are good citizens. We vote, we pay taxes—'

'This insanity will pass, Marty. Cool it,' Doug urged. But he couldn't erase his own anxiety about getting a conviction. He could hear the defense attorney now: '*These two young men – loving brothers – were out of their minds with grief. Their older sister murdered in the attack on the Twin Towers by vicious Arabs. They felt they had to avenge her horrible death.*'

'Mom will be cool,' Marty conceded. 'But I worry about Joe. He can be such a hothead. Will you talk to him? Make him understand these are weird times. He mustn't go shooting off his mouth!'

Conscious of the passing time, Doug left the hospital and returned to his car. As Assistant District Attorney – a part-time position in Weston – he would have a battle on his hands to win a conviction that would convince Marty Mohammad and his mother that justice could prevail in this town. Yet he was conscious of a compulsion to bring this off.

But as he drove towards his office – fighting yawns, because he'd slept little last night – he found his mind focusing on those brief moments when he was convinced he'd seen Karen walking out of a house right here in Weston.

When he came back home, he'd asked about Karen's whereabouts. Nobody had known where she had gone. After the ugly divorce – for which he was grateful – he'd told himself there'd never be another woman in his life. But last night, when he had seen Karen, he realized what he'd felt for her all those years ago still survived.

Can I make her understand what happened? Can there be a second chance for us?

His mind raced backward to the night he'd paced the hospital floor while Candy was being prepared for surgery . . .

'There's a problem,' the obstetrician explained. 'We'll have to do a C-section.'

'They'll be all right?' he asked in alarm. He had no illusions about this being a perfect marriage, but he clung to the prospect of becoming a father. A child would give meaning to his life. And in some odd fashion he felt that he would redeem himself in his parents' eyes. They were looking forward to becoming grandparents – though he sensed their distaste for Candy.

'Your wife will be fine,' the obstetrician said evasively.

'The baby?' Doug demanded, his throat tightening.

'We hope for the best.'

Doug paced about the reception area for hours. Leaping to attention each time someone strode down the hall from Surgery. And then – with the first pink-gray streaks of dawn lighting the sky – Candy's obstetrician came out to tell him.

'Your wife's fine,' he reassured Doug. 'I'm sorry. We did everything we could to save the baby.'

'Was it a boy or a girl?' he asked.

'A beautiful little girl,' the obstetrician said gently. 'But, as I told your wife, we were afraid we'd lose her.'

He felt an overwhelming grief. His daughter never had a chance, he mourned. *Why didn't Candy tell me?*

* * *

Doug pulled into the parking area behind the building where he maintained his modest office. He sat there, staring into space, remembering the day when he brought Candy home from the hospital. He'd thought she was hostile from grief, that she was distraught about the loss of their baby. How naive he had been – from the very beginning . . .

'Thank God, it's over,' she said with a defiant air.

'I know how you feel about losing the baby,' he began, but stopped at the sound of her derisive laughter.

'Do you think I wanted a kid? At my age?'

'It was our child.' He gazed at her in shock.

'Mine. Not yours.' Her eyes defied him to contradict this.

'You said that—that . . .' His mind was in chaos.

'I needed some poor sucker to take care of me. My parents would have thrown me out if they knew the truth. The bastard who made me pregnant was a married professor – and he meant to stay married.'

The following evening Candy had announced she wanted a divorce. '*Why should I stay married to a dumb law student dependent on his parents to support us?*' He'd been relieved to have their sham marriage over.

All right, get to the office, he ordered himself. He had a real estate closing at 11 a.m. Then he'd go over to the DA's office for a consultation about Marty's case. The DA wasn't exactly sanguine about winning a conviction. But Doug was developing a compulsion to win.

Those two creeps deserved to go to prison. And for the town's small group of Arab-Americans, it would be a sign that the democratic spirit survived, despite what had happened – one week ago today – at the World Trade Center, at the Pentagon, and on the hijacked plane that crashed in Pennsylvania.

Karen followed her schedule. Her phone would be in service by late afternoon. The cable company records indicated that cable service had never been disconnected. She'd unloaded her over-stuffed car trunk, brought out the cartons of books piled on the rear seat. Now – exhausted from her efforts – she sat on the sofa with the two local newspapers spread before her.

The job listings offered little that resembled her last position. Most of what she saw indicated low-paying jobs. Don't jump at the first available job-opening, she cautioned herself yet again. She'd done that for years before she landed a good one at the company.

While the rent here was tiny compared to what she would have been forced to pay in New York, even in the outer boroughs, the jobs listed provided little above minimum. No matter how carefully she'd budget, she couldn't live on that.

Had she jumped too fast in renting this apartment? No, her mind rejected. Lisa had warned her that the number of available apartments was small. '*In today's economy most singles live at home with their parents. And young marrieds all want a house.*'

Doug still lived in his family's house – just a few blocks from here. Lisa said his family had retired to Arizona because of his father's emphysema. Did he stay on there with the thought that he and his wife might reconcile? Perhaps for the sake of their child? Doug had always been so warm – he'd make a wonderful father, she thought involuntarily. He'd seemed warm, she taunted herself. How wrong she'd been about him!

Why am I thinking about Doug? He was two people – one who loved me and I loved, and one who was a liar and a cheat who walked out on me with a few brutal words. How can I have any feeling for him now?

She glanced at her watch. Time to go over to Lisa's apartment for dinner. Lisa was her lifeline. Lisa would help her pull her life together again.

* * *

'I didn't see a single ad that was worth a reply,' Karen told Lisa as they settled down to a hastily thrown together spaghetti and salad dinner. 'I'll pick up both newspapers first thing in the morning. I gather there's no employment agency in town?'

'Only an informal deal each morning where contractors and landscape people pick up day laborers.' But Lisa showed no indication of pessimism. 'You didn't expect to walk into town and find a decent job the next day.'

'I'll hold out for a week or ten days,' Karen decided. 'If nothing real shows up by then, I'll take whatever I can find. At least, I'll have some money coming in each week. I'll keep looking for something that can keep me afloat.' She could hang on for a while with what she had in reserve, Karen reasoned. She wouldn't sit on the panic button if a real job didn't surface right away.

Karen tensed at the sound of fire trucks racing through in the early evening. She felt sick – remembering how many firemen were missing, believed dead, at the World Trade Center. Down there, the fires were still smoldering.

'Frozen yogurt for dessert?' Lisa asked and chuckled reminiscently. 'Remember the great desserts Mom used to give us on special occasions?'

'Frozen yogurt is fine,' Karen approved. In the years after high school she'd become what Greg had good-humoredly called a health-food nut. 'Especially if it's low fat.'

'Oh, I wouldn't consider anything else.' Lisa laughed. 'Howie got me on that kick. He—' Lisa paused as the phone rang. 'Always at dinner—' She got up from her chair with a shrug. 'That's why Howie insists we eat out those nights when he's free – or we cook together at his place.' She reached to pick up the phone. 'Hello.' Her face tightened as she listened. 'Sophie, are you sure?' Lisa listened, looking suddenly anxious. 'No, don't go over there! Let me talk with her. I'll get back to you.' She paused for a moment. 'Sophie, I think it would be wise for you to stay home. Let me talk with Minna. I'll call you later.'

'Trouble?' Karen asked.

'A fire just broke out at a small pizza place off Main Street. It's owned by an Arab-American family. The mother just called Sophie. She was hysterical – the family thinks it was arson.'

'A pizza place is a prime target for a fire,' Karen said, almost defensively. 'Why do they suspect arson?'

'Because they smelled gasoline in the storage room where it started. The family's been here since 1897! And some ignorant bastard wants to run them out of town!'

'People are scared. It wouldn't happen in normal times.'

'It shouldn't happen at any time.' Lisa seemed involved in some inner debate. 'Karen, I shouldn't run out on you like this . . .'

'Lisa, I understand,' Karen insisted. 'It's part of your job. You run – I'll clear away the table, do the dishes.'

'Technically, it's not my job – they're not my clients. But in this situation I kind of consider the whole Arab-American community my client.'

'It'll take me a while to accept that not every Arab is a terrorist,' Karen acknowledged. 'But right now – after what happened a week ago – I can't do that.'

Doug sat tight-lipped and impatient in the night court where the arraignments were being held. Damn, it was hot – and the air-conditioning sucked. Glancing about, he noted the usual collection of drug cases, pimps, prostitutes – everyone stirring restlessly in the heatwave that had descended on the town. A larger crowd than normal, including uninvolved spectators. He spied Sophie, sitting erect and defensive at the rear. He lifted a hand and waved to her.

The Henderson brothers case was scheduled for the last of this session, he reminded himself. The 'star' position, he taunted in silence. The case was eliciting more than normal attention for assault charges – but that was because of the situation.

The DA had made it clear to him again – in their brief conversation before the arraignments began.

'Look, let's be realistic. Don't knock yourself out on this case. No jury is going to convict those two kids. Maybe they'll go on to a grand jury hearing – maybe not. But the grand jury is sure to throw it out.'

He didn't mean to allow that to happen, he promised himself. Those two young bastards had beat the hell out of Marty – for no reason at all. Everybody in the current administration was playing footsie with the others.

The two Henderson boys claimed they'd beat Marty up because of their sister's dying in the Twin Towers attack – caused by Arabs. Their sister had moved to New York four years ago, Doug recalled, because she wanted nothing to do with her father and brothers – always on the borderline of trouble.

In truth, did their beating up Marty have something to do with the case he was handling for Sophie and the three other property owners she'd brought along with her? Had they been hired to frighten her? The Sunshine people – the supermarket syndicate – was damn anxious to have their offer for the four properties accepted. All four refused.

Damn it, they were right to refuse. The offer was far below market value – and Sunshine needed that acreage for a parking area. The syndicate hinted at having condemnation proceedings put through – but there was no way Hank Fredericks would allow that to happen until after the election. It could lose him a lot of votes.

Unwarily, Doug remembered his near encounter with Karen. Had she seen him? He'd told himself he must banish her from his mind and heart. No doubt in his mind – she felt only contempt for the way he'd treated her.

God, he must have been the most naive 21-year-old in history to be roped in that way by Candy! He'd buried himself in work all these years – telling himself he could survive without Karen in his life because he must. But now she was here in Weston – and all the old feelings obsessed him.

He heard the Henderson brothers case called, ordered himself to snap into action. He was conscious of the undercurrent of excitement among the spectators. There was a lot of local interest in this case. All associated with the attack on September 11th.

Cal and Bart Henderson were high school dropouts who occasionally worked at odd jobs. He realized with disdain that they'd become heroes to a segment in this town. They were fighting what that contingent considered 'the enemy.'

Doug knew the DA was furious at him for fighting to have the Henderson brothers held for a grand jury hearing. Damn, how could they not be held, considering the case.

Still battered from the beating, Marty took the stand.

'They called me a stinking Arab – a murderer of Americans,' Marty said, fighting for calm because he'd been instructed to be cool on the stand. 'And then they beat me up.'

Doug took satisfaction in the judge ordering that Cal and Bart be held for a grand jury hearing. He knew the judge would face repercussions for this verdict. But not everybody in the administration was corrupt.

He made a point of walking with Marty and Sophie to her 11-year-old Dodge Spirit.

'We're going to put up a hard fight,' he promised. 'Those creeps need to be put away.'

'Mom had a call from the supermarket people,' Marty told him. *They should have called me. I'm representing the four families. They're a slimy crew.* 'They said this was their final offer. They hinted that after the election they'd probably drop it. Figuring with Fredericks re-elected and safely in office again, he'd condemn the property.'

'We have to fight to throw him out of office.' Doug's face tightened. 'I'm betting that Tony Mendoza is elected.'

But some of his conviction was ebbing away. What

happened down in New York on September 11th high-lighted what some voters were saying. That Tony Mendoza was not a 'real American.'

Eleven

Karen ordered herself to focus on job hunting. She'd thought she was coming back to a small, serene town – but was any town serene at this point? The fire at the pizza place had proven to be arson. The two responsible for beating up Marty Mohammed were being held for trial. She tried to ignore the ugly stories that were reported in the two local newspapers – about the feelings of some residents towards the town's Arab-American community, plus the rumblings of an election that was becoming increasingly vitriolic.

Each evening she clung to the latest news on TV about the World Trade Center disaster. All hope for rescues had been abandoned. Now it was just a search for bodies. But there'd been no doubt in her mind when she fled Manhattan that Greg and Michelle and Frank, and others missing from the company, were gone. And each night she awoke at intervals in a sweat – emerging from a new nightmare about those awful last days in Manhattan.

She'd written, but Jackie hadn't replied. Jackie was involved in getting her life back on track. Their lives had crossed paths for a few days. That's all that was meant to be. Come Christmas, Karen thought, they'd probably exchange Christmas cards.

Each morning now she bought the day's edition of *The Star* and *The Sentinel*. She'd worked up a resumé. Lisa had made copies for her. But interviews for the few office jobs were futile. '*I'm sorry – you're overqualified. You wouldn't be happy with us.*'

Meaning, she understood, that they were looking for someone just out of school, happy with an entry level salary. And she shied from accepting a $7-an-hour job at a bookstore, as a cashier in a restaurant, as a salesperson in a women's specialty shop. Still, by the end of the second week she was growing anxious.

She'd met Lisa for lunch several times in the past two weeks. Lisa apologized that her evenings were claimed either by special meetings called because of the situation in town or by Howie. But tonight Howie was going to be out of town. She and Lisa would have dinner. This time at her apartment.

The table was set in the tiny dining alcove. She'd planned a menu that could be thrown together in 15 minutes: salmon steaks, broccoli, baked potatoes (long in the oven), and a bread pudding with bourbon sauce prepared earlier. The dessert had been inspired by Amy Lansing, who'd served her this one rainy evening – and later provided the recipe.

She was grateful to have Amy Lansing for her landlady, Karen told herself while she moved about the apartment preparing dinner. Amy was so friendly – without being intrusive. Most evenings Amy was out at meetings – dealing with the mayoral election or the problems facing the Arab-American community or having dinner with friends.

Amy had reminded her that she'd be able to vote in the November elections if she registered immediately. She'd never missed voting, Karen thought with pride – and remembered how her mother had never bothered to vote. Not once in her life. '*Why should I bother to vote? What does my one vote count?*'

She was frustrated by the way Doug crept into her thoughts at unwary intervals. But she was forever encountering something in the newspapers about him and his role in the coming election. *The Star* vilified him. *The Sentinel* made him sound like the local hero.

The doorbell rang. Lisa got off at a reasonable hour today, she thought and hurried to the door.

'Surprise, surprise, I'm on time.' Lisa extended an aluminum-wrapped parcel. 'I saw Sophie this morning. She insisted on digging into her freezer and giving me some loot. Here's her exotic chicken and couscous specialty. Store it in the freezer until you're ready to use it. Then just throw it in the microwave and voilà, dinner in a few minutes.'

'Thanks. I'll put the salmon steaks on the grill, steam the broccoli. Come out to the kitchen and talk to me while I work.'

'Oh, slaving over a hot stove,' Lisa drawled. 'And all for me.'

'You work so hard – but you love it.' Karen prodded Lisa towards the kitchen.

'Yeah,' Lisa admitted. 'I bitch a lot – but it's what I want to do with my life. So – what happened today in the job market?'

'Zilch.' Karen sighed. 'I may have to take one of those "I can't live on that salary" jobs for a while.'

'I know of a temporary job.' A note of caution crept into Lisa's voice. 'Sophie runs a very smart gift shop on Main Street. She told me her saleswoman – with her since she opened the shop – quit this morning. Terrified when a group of young teenagers threw eggs at the display windows and yelled ethnic insults. I know Sophie would be delighted if you'd fill in. She's sure Nadine will come back as soon as the situation cools down.'

Karen hesitated. *Will the situation cool down?* 'Maybe for a couple of weeks,' she hedged. 'But if something else comes up . . .'

'Sophie will understand.' Lisa glowed. 'That's great. Sophie was fearful she'd have to close the shop for a while. She can't handle it alone.'

But that doesn't mean I'll feel at ease working for an Arab employer. Not with the TV news-shows flashing constant reminders of the Arab attackers of the Twin Towers. Not with Osama bin Laden's face popping up everywhere.

Karen had arrived with Lisa at Sophie Mohammed's shop with trepidation, but almost immediately she'd found herself drawn to this lovely, soft-spoken woman. Lisa had told her that Sophie was an educated woman. In the days of the Shah – before the Ayatollah Khomeini and his followers drove the Shah from Iran and formed the Islamic Republic – women in wealthy families were provided with a fine education.

'Sophie, everything in the shop is always so beautiful,' Lisa told her and turned to Karen. 'People always come here to buy special gifts. I must run now.' She reached to hug Sophie. 'I want you to promise me you'll stop being fearful each time somebody comes into the store. We've had a few bad days – but the madness is over.'

Sophie smiled, but her eyes were somber. 'Thank you for bringing me Karen.'

'A few crazies make everyone seem bad,' Karen comforted Sophie. 'At least, for a little while.'

'You two be good,' Lisa said, determined to be cheerful. 'Talk to you later.'

Karen gazed about the shop in admiration. 'This would be a beautiful shop even in the finest sections of Manhattan.'

'I hope we have no more trouble.' Sophie shuddered. 'I still can't believe Marty was beaten up – just because he's of Arab descent. I can't believe the graffiti – and the arson at the pizza restaurant.'

'These things happen in the first days after an awful disaster.' Karen clutched at Lisa's assessment of the situation. 'But life goes back to normal.' Karen struggled to sound confident. *I don't believe that. How can life go back to normal after what's happened?*

'Marty is so upset. He's talked to me about what happened to Japanese-Americans after Pearl Harbor.' Sophie clenched her hands into two small fists. 'How they were herded into internment camps – to live behind barbed-wire fences for four years. Karen, is that going to happen to us?'

'No,' Karen rejected, recoiling from the vision of Sophie Mohammed in such circumstances. 'That's a period in American history that was shameful. We won't let it happen again.'

'Last evening was my night to volunteer at the Tony Mendoza campaign headquarters. I went,' Sophie said with an air of defiance. 'But I felt like an intruder.'

'Mrs Mohammed – Sophie.' Karen corrected herself because Sophie had told her, 'I'm Sophie to everybody in town.' 'I'm sure they're grateful for your help.'

'But I make them feel uncomfortable.' Sophie sighed. 'How do I make them understand that I'm a real American – just as they are?'

Karen returned to her apartment at the end of the day with a sense of becoming part of the town again. She was uneasy at the internal conflicts. But she had an apartment and a job – though the job was temporary. She would survive.

After breakfast at the Main Street Café on this early October morning, Doug headed for the Mohammeds' house. He knew Sophie would still be home. She opened the shop at 10 a.m. When they talked yesterday evening, she'd sounded as though she was fighting panic. She mustn't give in to the demands of the Sunshine people.

Of course, it wasn't just the Mohammeds' house that was at stake. Three other neighbors had joined with Sophie in hiring him to fight for them. All four families rejected – rightly – the payments offered for their property. But Sunshine must have the three acres involved for their parking area. The building was almost ready for occupancy. Sunshine hadn't expected this long a battle to acquire the needed property. They couldn't open until the parking area was set up.

Recalling Ted Ramsey's words, Doug winced: *'Hell, Doug, what are they bitching about? We're offering them market value.'* Market value 25 years ago. Every real estate broker in town knew the price the syndicate was offering was a joke. They were attempting blatant robbery.

But he was apprehensive. Ted was a strong supporter of Hank Fredericks. He came right out and said that – after he'd been re-elected – the Mayor would see to it that the property was condemned – and available at whatever the supermarket offered. How much had the supermarket – a chain – contributed to the Mayor's campaign fund?

The case had been pushed into the background by what happened in New York and Washington on September 11th. And, of course, the Mayor wanted to keep it on a back burner until after the election. He recoiled from the prospect of Fredericks winning another term.

Tony Mendoza was for everything that was right for Weston. He ridiculed Fredericks' plan to freeze the teaching staff from kindergarten through 12th grade 'because that's the only way to lower taxes, put money back into over-taxed hands.' Tony even promised to fight to raise the minimum wage in Weston to $6.50 an hour.

Driving past a house with a red-rose-covered trellis, he thought involuntarily of Karen's passion for red roses. For an instant he considered sending her a bunch of long-stemmed red roses – as a silent apology for destroying their dreams all those years ago.

A dozen times a day – for no real reason – he found his mind darting back through the years to those perfect few months when they were so sure their lives would be forever entwined. And then – due to a brief encounter with Candy – their future together was denied.

All at once Doug realized he'd been in such deep thought

he was about to pass the turn-off that would take him to the Mohammed house. He made a sharp right.

At the small, white cinder-block contemporary made colorful by the presence of neat circles of late summer–early autumn flowers, Doug swung into the driveway. Before he reached the front door, Sophie had flung it wide, and she stood there with a welcoming smile.

'I have fresh coffee made,' Sophie greeted him. 'And baklava just out of the oven. I know it's early in the morning for such sweetness, but—'

'Sophie, when could I resist your baklava?'

Without discussing the business at hand – or Sophie's fear of another anti-Arab outbreak in town – they settled at the table in the cozy kitchen.

'I know you're anxious about the house,' Doug began.

'I worry about something else this morning,' she interrupted. 'I didn't tell you when we spoke last evening.' She'd just told Doug she needed to talk with him.

'What's bothering you, Sophie?'

'It's Joe.' Her hand trembled as she lifted the dainty coffee cup to her mouth.

'Trouble on the job?' He knew Marty had brought Joe in on the construction job at the edge of town where several local Arab-Americans were employed. And Joe was a hothead sometimes.

'He's talking crazy – ever since Marty was beat up – and the things happened. He said – when we sat down to supper last night – and Marty and I were stunned!'

'Sophie, what did he say?' Doug prodded.

'He has such rage in him. He's always looked up to Marty as – what's the phrase . . .?' She squinted in thought for a moment. 'Role model,' she pinpointed. 'When he saw what had happened to Marty, he wanted to go out and kill somebody. And now . . .' She closed her eyes for a moment in anguish. 'Now he says – he says he wants to go to Afghanistan – to fight with the Taliban. He says he hates Americans. Doug, he was born in this country!'

'He'll never get to Afghanistan,' Doug assured her. 'Does he even have a passport?'

'Joe's never been out of this country. But when he talks about Osama bin Laden being a hero, I feel sick,' Sophie whispered. 'Bin Laden is using our religion to justify what happened at the World Trade Center and the Pentagon and on that hijacked plane that went down in Pennsylvania. Islam is a peaceful religion. How do we make everyone understand that?'

'People are working on that – but it'll take time.'

'Please talk to Joe. Make him realize he's talking crazy. He thinks you're a wonderful man, Doug. He'll listen to you.'

'I'll talk to him. He's still working on the same construction job with Marty?'

Sophie nodded. 'I wanted him to go back to college this year, but he insisted on taking a year off – to earn money. Like Marty,' she said tenderly. 'Joe and Marty are good boys. I can't bear what's happening to them.'

'I'll talk to Joe,' Doug said again. 'I'll tell Marty to talk to him. But there's no chance that he'll be able to leave this country to go and fight with bin Laden. That I can promise you.'

Doug parked at the construction site where Marty and Joe worked. The sprawling warehouse was near completion, he noted. That job would soon be over. In the current climate would Marty and Joe run into problems lining up another job?

He glanced about for the site superintendent, approached him, exchanged a few casual words.

'I need to talk to Joe Mohammed for a couple of minutes. Okay?' he asked with a persuasive smile.

'Yeah – for a few minutes,' he stipulated. 'The boss wouldn't like it to become a tea party.'

Joe was startled at seeing him here, Doug realized. Play

it cool. Sometimes Joe was a hothead, but he was good kid. He was 19 – being a hothead went with the territory.

'Hi.' Joe sounded wary. *He knows his mother sent me over to talk to him.*

'You know why I'm here.' Doug's tone was casual.

'Mom forgets sometimes that I'm a grown man.' But Joe was defensive.

'She knows you're upset at all the craziness that's been happening here in town. She doesn't want you to go off on some tangent that'll backfire. But be realistic. There's no way you'll be able to go to Afghanistan.' *No point in telling him that Osama bin Laden is a paranoid terrorist who's been disowned by his whole family.*

'I'll get out.' Joe was grim. 'By way of Canada or Cuba. We don't belong in this country. We'll end up in internment camps – like the Japanese-Americans after World War Two. I see it coming!'

'It won't come,' Doug insisted. 'Americans won't allow it.'

'Hey, I gotta get back to work.' Joe brushed him off. 'See ya.'

Doug headed for the office. His mind in mental debate. No way could Joe get out of the country in present circumstances – but how could he be sure?

Stop by the DA's office for a quick conference, he ordered himself. He was relieved that the grand jury hearing of the two who had beat up Marty was scheduled for after the November 6th election day. But he was uneasy that the DA hinted that they had a weak case. Hell, Marty identified the two creeps! There were hospital records that showed his injuries.

The conference lasted longer than he'd anticipated. The DA was playing games with the Mayor, he interpreted. Fredericks wanted the two creeps cleared.

Behind the wheel of the car again, Doug debated about heading directly to the office. No. He dialed the office on his cell phone.

'Good morning, the law office of—' Olivia's effervescent voice came to him.

'Livvy, I'll be a little late this morning.'

Go over to Sophie's shop – she must be there by now. Tell her he'd spoken with Joe. Urge her to be cool about this whole thing. He couldn't see Joe getting out of the country. Not with security at the level it was reaching now.

Twelve

Karen waited at the door of the shop in the early October sunlight. Greg used to tease her about always being just a bit early. She glanced at her watch. It was 9:51 a.m. Sophie would be here at any moment.

She'd been working for Sophie such a little while, she mused, yet she felt as though she'd been here for weeks. She was grateful to be occupied during the day. She dreaded the evenings alone in the apartment. When would she learn not to spend agonizing hours watching the endless parade of TV news?

Lisa had tried to bring her into the volunteer scene. '*Karen, these last few weeks of Tony Mendoza's campaign are so important. And we need every volunteer we can dig up.*'

How could she involve herself in the Mendoza campaign? Doug was his top advisor. She wasn't ready to run into Doug yet. She needed time to gear herself for a possible encounter. But for as long as possible let her avoid it.

He was divorced, she reminded herself. Lisa's words echoed in her mind. '*He and his wife divorced before their first anniversary.*' *Had he walked out on their child the way he'd walked out on her? But stop this absurd habit of thinking about Doug. He's out of my life. I'd be insane to think of resurrecting something that died.*

Her face lit up. Sophie was approaching. Would Sophie think she was being intrusive to have worked up what could be a monthly or bi-monthly newsletter to regular customers?

But Sophie had confided that she was anxious – in the face of the nastiness towards Arab-Americans in Weston – to reach out to those customers.

'Karen, I'll have a key made up for you.' Sophie smiled apologetically. 'You shouldn't have to wait outside for me this way.'

'I was just here a couple of minutes,' Karen dismissed.

'I brought along fresh-made baklava for our tea break.' Sophie unlocked the door, pushed it open. 'Most of the time I'm so good about staying with a healthy diet – I watch sweets and fat and cholesterol.' She allowed herself a chuckle. 'I told them over at the health food store I thank them in my prayers every night for opening up here in town. I used to drive thirty-eight miles each way to my other health food store.'

'Where is it?' Karen was elated to discover the presence of a store in Weston. 'One of the things I miss most about Manhattan is my health food store that was just around the corner on Second Avenue.'

'It's right off Main Street at Linwood Avenue,' Sophie told her. 'Marty and Joe tease me about eating veggie burgers all the time – they can't believe I really like them. Just the way they tease me for waking up so early in the morning – but it's a habit, from the days when they were in school and there was much to do before I got them off and then myself to the shop.'

'I think it's wonderful how you've brought them up on your own.'

'Life is never easy for most of us.' Sophie's smile was philosophical. 'We must treasure the small, happy times.'

'You were talking yesterday about how anxious you were about people continuing to come to the shop,' Karen said, fighting self-consciousness. 'Well – I had an idea – about a newsletter.'

'Oh, Karen, tell me!' Sophie glowed.

Haltingly, Karen explained her proposal. She reached

into her purse to pull out the two pages she'd worked out on the computer last night.

'I remembered what you'd told me about new items that had just come into the shop – and some that you expected shortly. This is a rough idea – something for you to play with.'

Sophie read the material Karen offered. Then she lifted her eyes and looked at Karen. 'This is great! You have a special gift. We'll use it just as you've written it. Maybe we'll use part of it in an ad. If you agree, of course.'

'Sophie, it's yours – to use any way you like.' Karen felt a shaky pleasure in Sophie's delight.

'You were an advertising executive in New York,' Sophie guessed.

'No. Until three years ago I worked at all kinds of low-level jobs,' Karen confided. 'Then I went from administrative assistant to writing market reports and sales letters.' She was suddenly assaulted by horrendous recall. 'I should have been at my office on September 11th – it was a miracle that I didn't die that day.'

'You were meant to survive.' Sophie's eyes were tender. 'I'm not a truly religious person,' she admitted. 'But I believe in these things. Something good is out there awaiting you.'

Karen glanced up with a welcoming smile when she heard the door open. And then she froze. Doug had just walked into the shop.

'Doug, how nice,' Sophie began and stopped short as she saw the startled exchange between Karen and him.

'Hi, Karen.' Doug's voice echoed a mixture of astonishment and anticipation.

'Hi.' Karen managed to make this an impersonal greeting.

'You know each other,' Sophie effervesced. But her eyes were full of questions. 'Two of my favorite people.'

'We had a class together at college in our senior year,' Karen said after a moment. 'That was before you moved to Weston.'

'I talked to Joe,' Doug told Sophie and hesitated.

'You can talk in front of Karen,' Sophie assured him. 'Did he toss all the craziness at you?'

'Sophie, he's nineteen and upset. With reason.' Doug's upset, Karen noticed. He didn't expect to walk in here and find me. He ought to be upset – after what he did all those years ago. 'But there's practically no chance of him getting to Afghanistan with the security that's being put in place. Play it cool, Sophie. Let Joe rant. That's as far as it'll go.'

'I'm afraid.' Sophie's voice was uneven. 'I think of what the bin Laden camps are doing to so many young people. Making them believe that suicide will lead them to a life in Paradise.' Her voice stronger now, contemptuous.

'Joe was born in this country – he's never been to the Middle East.' Doug made a point of focusing on Sophie. *I've shaken him up. He knows I've met the other Doug – the one people in this town have probably never met.* 'He's been hurt by what's happening, but he'll come out of it.'

'Every morning I wake up with thanks to God for those women Lisa brought together to act as escorts for those of us who're afraid to leave our houses. I was afraid, too,' Sophie confessed, 'but I'm too stubborn to let anyone know. For so long I've thought of myself as an American. Now, to others in town I'm an Arab-American – and that makes me an alien.'

'Sophie, we're all hyphenated Americans. I'm both Polish-American and Irish-American. My grandparents on my mother's side were Polish. My grandparents on my father's side were Irish. Only native Americans have no hyphenated designations.'

This is the Doug I thought I knew. Of course, everybody in this town thinks he's a wonderful human being. This is the Doug they see.

'Do you think I should continue volunteering at campaign headquarters?' Sophie was ambivalent. 'I want to be helpful, but . . .' She gestured her confusion.

'We need you,' Doug said, his smile sympathetic. 'Don't be turned off if some stupid person appears uncertain about your loyalties. I know,' he continued, anticipating her retort. 'Some ignorant voices have been making ugly noises.'

'And actions,' she reminded him.

'We can't let a handful of voices blot out the voices of the majority,' Doug insisted. 'Most people in this town – in towns all over the country – understand that a small group of Arabs are guilty of heinous crimes. But they know most Arab-Americans are fine citizens who contribute to society.'

'I suppose I'm unnerved because so much is happening at once.' Sophie struggled for calm. 'I'll try to remember that I have many friends here. My customers are still coming into the shop.' She took a deep breath. 'Most of them . . .'

'I have to get to the office now.' Doug cast a troubled glance at Karen. 'You've come home to live?'

'For the moment.'

Be casual. Don't let him know I'm falling apart inside.

'It's good to see you.'

Karen saw the way Sophie's eyes followed Doug from the shop. She saw that Sophie suspected there'd been more than a casual relationship between Doug and her, but she was too polite to ask questions.

Is there enough space in this town for both Doug and me?

Business was slow in the shop throughout the day. People were too upset to think about shopping, Karen told herself. But Sophie kept herself busy. She re-arranged stock. She made lists of customers to receive their newly-devised newsletter. Repeatedly she thanked Karen for this effort.

For Karen the hours seemed endless. Her mind assaulted at unwary intervals by a replay of the encounter with Doug. His eyes told her he was eager to pick up where they'd left off all those years ago.

She felt a surge of guilt that she could allow Doug to invade her thoughts. Except for that murderous attack on the Twin Towers she'd be Greg's wife by now. Greg was so good for her. They could have had a real marriage. *How can I think about another man when Greg lies buried with all those others beneath the rubble at the World Trade Center? Except for Greg's insistence that I stay home, I'd be there with him now.* Yet, truantly, she remembered those ecstatic months with Doug.

Minutes before the shop was scheduled to close, the phone rang. Sophie called to her to pick up.

'Hello, The Oasis.'

'Hi,' Lisa greeted her. 'Howie's tied up at the hospital. I don't feel like cooking. Want to grab a simple dinner with me at the Main Street Diner?'

'I'd love it.'

'The store's closing soon?'

'In a few minutes,' Karen told her.

'Okay, let's head for the diner. Their dinners aren't fancy, but we can sit and yak as long as we like – and the coffee's good.'

'Meet you there.'

Twenty minutes later they sat across from each other in a booth at the rear. Even here, Karen thought subconsciously, there was a subdued air among the sprinkling of early diners. It was though every individual in the country was aware that their lives had been forever changed.

'You order one of two things here at dinner,' Lisa cautioned as a waiter approached. 'The roast chicken or the Greek salad.'

Karen and Lisa ordered. Karen was gearing herself to tell Lisa about the encounter with Doug. The moment she'd dreaded since she'd seen Doug emerging from a house across from her apartment in Weston.

'I have to rush off in about an hour,' Lisa warned as Karen was framing words in her head. 'I have to escort an

Arab-American woman to the support group. I've pulled
one together fast.' Her smile was wry. 'Everything has to
be fast these days. Her husband works as a dishwasher on
the evening shift here. In Afghanistan, he was an engineer
with graduate degrees.'

'That's rough.' Karen tensed. A montage of Arab faces
that dominated the newspapers darted across her mind. The
faces of those who had killed thousands of innocent civilians.

*I'm able to accept Sophie – yes. But how do we know
which Arab means to kill us along with himself – because
it's been drilled into his head that to die by killing Americans
is to buy a ticket to Paradise?*

'I'm having a rough time on providing escorts over the
weekend. You know, families are claiming women's atten-
tions.' Lisa paused. 'Karen, you have such a warm way
with people. Could you give a couple of hours over the
weekend? These women are terrified – they know what's
happening all over the country. People who aren't even
Arabs – Indians, Pakistanis.'

'It might help,' Karen said defensively, 'if these women
dressed to blend with the rest of us. I know,' she added
before Lisa could comment. 'Sophie dresses in Western
style – but not everyone does.'

'Sophie's son was attacked – and he wears the same
clothes as any kid in America his age. But if those women
want to observe Arab tradition, why shouldn't they wear
what they like? This is a free country. We don't ask Orthodox
Jews to throw away their yarmulkas. I don't hear anybody
objecting to African-American dreadlocks.'

'Lisa, I'm sorry – I know I shouldn't feel this way. But
you weren't in New York on the morning of September 11th.
You didn't see what happened when those planes slammed
into the Twin Towers. All those people died because Arabs
wanted them dead.' Karen's voice broke. 'I'm sorry. I know
it's wrong, but I look at Arab faces – and I'm terrified.'

Thirteen

Just as Karen parked by the house, she saw Amy charging down the path. The way Amy walked, and her grim expression, telegraphed her agitation.

'Karen, I'm so furious!'

'What's happened?' Karen pushed open the door and emerged from the car.

'There's been another fire. At a produce store run by an Arab-American family.' Amy sighed in exasperation. 'It's under control – but it was arson.'

'How awful!' Since September 11th any mention of fire unnerved her. The fires still smoldered at the World Trade Center.

'I'm going over to *The Sentinel* to talk with Mike Canfield. He's the publisher – and the editor.' Amy's face softened. 'Such a fine man. I called – he's there. We've got to stop this insanity. This was always a good town. I can't believe what's happening.'

Karen hesitated. 'Do they have any idea about who's responsible for the fire?'

'Not yet – but it'll come out. I hope whoever's doing this gets put away for life!'

'At least we know it can't be those two who're accused of beating up Marty Mohammed.' Cal and Bart Henderson were being held until the grand jury hearing.

'More of the same ilk.' Amy's eyes glittered with contempt. 'Where did we go so wrong that something so dastardly can be happening in our town? I'd better get over to *The Sentinel*. Mike's probably been at the paper since seven this morning.'

As Amy drove off to meet with Mike, Karen put her car into the garage and headed for her apartment. Sophie would be so upset about this second fire at an Arab-American property. For a moment she considered calling her. No, she rejected this thought. What could she say that would comfort Sophie?

Wearing a robe over her nightgown because the evening had become unseasonably cool, Karen sat before the television set and worked the remote – surfing between the local TV station and CNN, where news was constant. The local commentator was emphasizing the division in the town over the coming trial of the two who were accused of assaulting Marty Mohammed.

'The Mayor pleads for residents not to jump to conclusions,' the local TV newscaster reported. 'He warns against making unknown assumptions about the fire. He and the Fire Chief point out there's no real evidence that the two fires in question were arson. The fact that both were Arab-owned businesses could very well be a coincidence.'

In a spurt of indecision she flipped off the TV. She remembered what Lisa had said about Mayor Fredericks – about the corruption in his administration. He was trying to hush up these arson cases. That was wrong.

Lisa was spending as much time as she could manage on Tony Mendoza's campaign. '*Howie has such crazy hours, but he's putting in time, too. We've got to get Hank Fredericks out of office. He's destroying this town.*'

She felt a recurrent guilt, Karen acknowledged to herself, that she wasn't part of the local volunteering. Lisa, Sophie, Amy were all involved. If he were alive, Dad would be involved. Amy – probably lots of people – remembered him as being a fine citizen. A fine citizen was concerned about what was happening in his or her town.

The time back in high school – when she'd been so eager to work for Walter Mondale's presidential campaign – Mom had ridiculed her. Not even when Geraldine Ferraro was running as his vice-president – a woman! – would Mom bother to go out and vote. But enough of this – this wasn't the right time for her to be active in politics.

At last Karen decided to call it a night. These were the hours she dreaded – when she went to bed with the knowledge that sleep would be evasive. She'd try all the much-touted routines that were supposed to induce sleep. Eventually – from exhaustion – she'd drift off into troubled nightmares that relived those first ghastly days after the attack.

She awoke – as usual, without the need of the alarm clock – to the sound of rain pelting the windows. Her mind rushed back through the years to a rainy Saturday morning. The first time she and Doug had made love. She was still unnerved from the death of her father and the suicide of her mother – and Doug was her safe haven.

The two students who shared the apartment with Doug had gone home for the weekend. With charismatic charm he'd persuaded her to come to the apartment for dinner. *'I'll cook for you – show you my potential as a husband.'* They'd been seeing each other every possible moment for the past two months. But that was the first time he'd said in so many words that he meant for them to be together forever.

It had seemed so miraculous – in the time of her loss to find this new love. With Doug she'd felt a passion that simultaneously exhilarated and frightened her. What would she do if something awful happened and she lost him? And the 'something awful' happened – and she was devastated.

I mustn't fall into that trap again. I've lost Greg – I'm on my own. I can survive alone. There's no place in my life for Doug. Remember that.

94

Now she forced herself to prepare for the day – though she wasn't due at the shop for almost three hours. She ordered herself not to turn on the TV. No news this morning. It was time to move out of the cocoon to which September 11th had thrust her. Greg wouldn't want her to fall apart. He'd been her lifeline to sanity – but now it was time to stand on her own.

Lisa was right. She needed to be involved in something outside of herself. She ought to work for Tony Mendoza's election. Yet she recoiled from this. Doug was Mendoza's major advisor. He would always be underfoot.

She left the apartment in a heavy rain, headed for the shop almost an hour before she was due to arrive. Sophie had given her a key. She'd work on a logo for Sophie's newsletter, she told herself. Again, she thought of Sophie's anguish at this second case of arson. How many lives – beyond the 2,000 plus murdered – were to be destroyed?

Approaching the shop she stiffened in shock. *Who is that man coming through the door?* Then, moments later, she saw Sophie. It was all right. Sophie was smiling.

'Good morning,' the man greeted her and walked on.

'Good morning.' These days they always anticipated the worst, she rebuked herself and walked into the shop.

'I've hired a security guard,' Sophie told her. 'For a 12-hour shift, from 9 p.m. to 9 a.m. Marty persuaded me that it was the wise thing to do.'

'It's awful that such a thing is necessary.' How long could Sophie afford this expense? she wondered. How long would it be 'the wise thing to do'?

'There was another incident last night.' Sophie was groping for words. 'Bricks were thrown into a house. One grazed a little three-year-old in her crib.'

Karen turned cold. 'Is she all right?'

'She was lucky – just a slight concussion. When Marty and I heard about that, we knew we had to do something. Doug called me as soon as he heard. He said he's going to talk to the police about protection for us.' Sophie closed her eyes for a moment. 'I can't believe this is happening. I can't believe I'm feeling like a stranger in my own town.

Doug sat at the edge of his chair in the Police Chief's private office. He fought to conceal his rage. 'How can you say we can't provide protection for the Arab-Americans in town? A three-year-old child was almost killed last night!'

'It was a freakish accident.' Chief Reagan shifted papers on his desk, avoiding visual confrontation. 'Whoever threw the brick didn't mean to hurt anybody. It was just a moment of rage at what the Arabs are doing to this country.'

'We're allowing a lunatic fringe to threaten the lives of local citizens.' *Sophie's a sitting duck in her shop. And Karen's working there now. They need protection.* 'We have to get the message across to them that we won't tolerate such acts. Temporary police protection, Bill,' Doug cajoled. He felt sick at the prospect of violence being inflicted on Sophie or Karen.

'I don't have the manpower.' Reagan's eyes met Doug's now. 'We can't put our necks out for a handful of residents. We've got a town of almost eleven thousand people to protect.'

'Are you waiting for somebody to be murdered to recognize this problem?' Doug challenged. 'Wasn't it enough that Marty Mohammed was beaten up? They might have killed him if they hadn't seen people approaching and let him go.'

'Doug, these are crazy times. Those two boys were out of their minds with grief.' *God, I hate this pious attitude! Is this what I'm going to run into at the trial? "They were grieving – we have to forgive them".* 'Their only sister was killed by those Arab nuts. They weren't thinking straight.'

'Then maybe we need to form a private unit to provide night patrols.'

Reagan stiffened in wariness. 'No vigilante stuff, Doug. We won't allow that.'

'A civilian patrol to provide safety for those in danger.' Play it cool, he ordered himself. 'We'll come up with something.'

He left the Police Chief's office, headed for a meeting with the DA. He was getting nowhere, he thought in frustration, in pushing ahead the grand jury hearing of those two scumbags who beat up Marty. There was a conspiracy to hold it over until after the election. Hank Frederick's crowd didn't want this vendetta against the local Arab-Americans to be an issue in the election – because not everybody, thank God, was on their side.

At the wheel of his car, Doug paused to call his office. Livvy was coming in to finish up some work on that closing this afternoon, he remembered.

'Good morning, the office of—' Olivia's voice greeted him.

'Livvy, I'll be there in about forty minutes,' he broke in. 'Any word from the supermarket crew?' More stalling, he surmised impatiently. They wouldn't make a decent offer when they figured Fredericks would be re-elected and his zoning board would cut the property owners' throats.

'Not a whisper,' Olivia confirmed.

'Figures.' Doug sighed. They didn't want to take a chance on losing votes if they acted now. At this point the town was divided right down the middle.

Doug reached for the ignition key. Go on over and talk to the DA, he ordered himself. He had to make the effort, even though he was sure of the outcome. But his mind was straying from business.

Was Karen going to remain here in town? She'd sounded ambivalent. How could he make her understand how stupid he'd been to let Candy break them up? How could he make her realize that she'd never been totally out of his thoughts all these years? He'd fallen into the habit of working 70-hour weeks to divert his mind from the way he'd wrecked his life.

Can we ever get together again?

Fourteen

Karen returned from her lunch break to discover Sophie involved in an agitated phone conversation. She remained at a distance to provide Sophie with privacy, but she felt anxious.

'Marty, he does such crazy things! I'm afraid.' Sophie's voice – always so quiet – was shrill. 'Joe left the house minutes after you.' Sophie paused as she listened to Marty. 'I know. Doug said he'll never get out of the country – but how can we be sure?' She listened again. 'Yes, my darling, I'll see you at dinner.' She put down the phone, then stared into space.

'Sophie, are you all right?' Karen was solicitous.

'That son of mine. Joe.' Sophie sighed. 'He didn't show up on the job. His boss contacted Marty.' She gestured in frustration. 'I know – he's run off. He can't live with what's happening here in this town – all across the country. When they beat up Marty, he just cracked. He's talking about going to Afghanistan – to join up with the Taliban.'

'He'll come home,' Karen said with confidence. 'The borders are being watched as never before. There's no way he can get to Afghanistan.'

'What is wrong with these young men?' Sophie flared. 'They profess to be dedicated Muslims. But there's nothing in the Koran that allows violence against innocent people. And these so-called martyrs . . .' She grimaced in distaste. 'The Koran forbids suicide. It's a sin. The radical Muslims

99

start with the very young – kindergarten children – and they teach them to hate. All they know is to hate Americans and Jews.'

'But Joe isn't like that,' Karen objected gently.

'I taught him better. He'd had a decent education – and God willing, he'll have more. How could he become infested with such rage?'

'He'll come home, Sophie,' Karen insisted. 'He loves you. He loves Marty. He couldn't bear seeing Marty hurt – he'll come out of it.'

'I hope – I pray. Karen, what's happening to our world?'

Doug was relieved that the early afternoon closing went through without a hitch. He needed to sit down with Tony and talk to him about setting up the private patrol he'd thrown at the Police Chief. It was necessary, damn it!

Instinct told him, too, that this might convince voters on the fence to vote for Tony. A civilian patrol would prove that the Mendoza campaign was concerned about the safety of its citizens. And this was a time of much anxiety among many. Let them know they were voting for a candidate that cared for people.

His face relaxed for a moment. It was wonderful the way people – especially the young – were responding to the needs of the country. Reports said that college students were all eager to secure jobs after graduation that contributed to the country's needs. No longer was it 'How much money can I earn?' It was 'What can I do to serve my country?'

Arriving at headquarters – always especially active on Saturdays, he felt a surge of pride. A full house this afternoon. Their volunteers were dedicated. They must win this election, get rid of the corruption that had been building through these past eight years.

He was conscious of an undercurrent of tension as he walked inside. Gloria, Tony's press chief, charged towards him.

'Doug, have you heard the radio in the last hour?'

'I was at a closing.' Warning signals shot up in his head. 'What's happening?'

'Mayor Fredericks,' Gloria said tightly. 'He's announced that because of the "state of war" he's issuing an order that all residents of foreign birth register at the Town Hall. They'll be fingerprinted and given photo ID.' She took a deep breath. 'That includes Tony.'

'He can't do that!' Doug gaped in disbelief. 'That's illegal!'

'He says we're at war.' Gloria's voice was scathing. 'He means to protect us against our unseen enemies. He claims that a local man – a foreigner – has taken off to fight in Afghanistan – with bin Laden.' *Joe must have shot off his mouth. But Joe isn't a foreigner – he was born in this country.* 'He's one of them, Fredericks claims – the fanatics who attacked this country.' She took a deep breath. 'But we know, of course, that he's doing this to discredit Tony.'

'Doug!' Tony called to him from the doorway of the office they shared. 'Have you ever heard such nonsense?'

'I suspect that most of our "residents of foreign birth" are American citizens,' Doug pointed out. 'Like you – and the Arab-American families in town and many others. He can't do that. Let's go over and talk to Mike at *The Sentinel*.' Unexpectedly, Doug chuckled. 'Tony, this just might cost Hank Fredericks the election. He's crossed the line this time.'

'Don't be so sure,' Tony warned. 'We've got a lot of scared folks here in town. Don't be so sure.'

'We'll take it to court,' Doug said. 'Fredericks can't get away with this.'

Sundays were the worst days, Karen thought as she lay in bed and anticipated the empty hours ahead. It was absurd the way she clung to the TV set when she was home, she jeered inwardly. Why must endless programs begin with those horrible pictures of the Twin Towers in flames? It was torment to watch. A torment to hear the dreadful statistics over and over again.

She heard church bells ringing in the distance. Startled, she turned to inspect the night-table clock. It was past 9 a.m. She never stayed in bed this late. But she'd tossed in wakefulness until the first pink streaks of dawn crept between the drapes.

She'd spend the morning cleaning the apartment, doing laundry, she decided. Today she was to go to Lisa's apartment for a very late lunch. *'It's time you and Howie met. He works at a storefront clinic from nine to one on Sundays – and he always gets stuck for a bit. What about lunch around two thirty?'*

She wouldn't turn on the TV this morning. Focus on cleaning, doing the laundry. The morning would pass. She debated for a moment about running downtown to pick up the Sunday newspapers. No – only more bad news. By 2 p.m. she'd finished her chores. In fifteen minutes she'd leave for Lisa's apartment. Lisa had insisted there was no need to bring anything. All right, no food. But she'd be extravagant – and take red roses.

Arriving at Lisa's house, she heard the sound of convivial voices inside. For an instant she was tense. Lisa wasn't making this a party, was she? *I'm not ready to face a bunch of strangers.*

She rang the bell and waited. She heard music – something by Beethoven. Why couldn't she ever remember the names of pieces she loved? Like this.

The door opened. A casually handsome, dark-haired man in his early 30s smiled down at her.

'Hi.' He radiated warmth. 'You must be Karen.'

'Right. And you're Howie.'

'Come on in. Lisa's been cooking up a storm. She's trying to win me over,' he drawled. 'She's learned to make gefilte fish. I admitted my mother bought it in jars.'

'I bought it at Citarella's on Broadway and 75th Street in Manhattan,' Karen recalled. On sight she liked Howard Rosen.

Howie's face lit up. 'I lived for three years on 74th and West End when I was going to med school. Lisa,' he called, 'you didn't tell me Karen's a New Yorker.'

'She was born and raised right here.' Lisa came forward to receive the roses. 'Oh, they're gorgeous! Let me put them in water.' She detoured into the kitchenette, reached into a cabinet for a vase. Karen and Howie lingered at the entrance.

'A lot of us go away to school but a fair amount of us come back.' Howie's grin was complacent.

'You grew up here in Weston?' Karen searched her mind for some recall.

'Not high school,' Howie said. 'My mother had a long bout with cancer – I went to boarding school those years.'

'She's fine now,' Lisa reported. 'Very active here in town.'

'This is interesting. The three of us here all spent time living in Manhattan. But we've all come back. Plus Doug, my roommate in Manhattan for those years. Oh, you may know him. Doug Madison.'

Karen was startled, cast a swift glance at Lisa, running water into the vase. Almost imperceptibly, Lisa shook her head.

'Yes, I knew Doug – at college.'

'He's great for this town. I doubt that Tony Mendoza would be running for mayor if he didn't have Doug right there fighting for him.' Again, Karen's eyes sought Lisa's. More forcefully Lisa shook her head. *Howie doesn't know about Doug and me.* 'It was Doug who shoved me into starting our weekend storefront clinic for families with no health insurance.'

'Did you see the article in *The Sentinel* about our great mayor planning to make all foreign-born residents register and be fingerprinted?' Lisa asked with distaste. 'Including his opponent in the election?'

'I didn't get today's newspapers.' Karen struggled to appear casual.

'He won't get away with it.' Howie's voice was firm. '*The Sentinel* will rip the whole idea to shreds. Besides, I talked with Doug this morning. He's sure they can stop it.' Howie sighed. 'I wish to hell Doug would stop running himself to death. It's as though he's afraid to be idle for a minute.' Howie frowned in thought. 'I suppose he never got over that rotten marriage he was dragged into. He never told me – but I got it out of one of his college roommates.'

'Oh?' Karen's heart was pounding.

'Howie, you sound like an old *yenta*,' Lisa scolded.

Karen hesitated. Instinct told her to drop this – but a yearning to know overwhelmed instinct. 'I'd heard he was married – and they had a child.'

'Not that I know of.' Howie shrugged. 'If he had a kid, Doug would talk about him – or her.'

'Howie, set the table,' Lisa ordered with mock sternness. 'Do I have to do everything around here?'

On Monday morning – early as usual – Karen saw the night watchman taking off. What an awful expense for Sophie, she worried. Was anything happening with that night patrol Lisa had talked about last evening?

'Nice morning,' the night watchman greeted her. 'Hope we're not moving into another hot spell this late in the year.'

'The weathercasters talk about temperatures in the low 80s,' Karen told him. 'But we always have one last gasp this time of year.'

'What do they call it?' He squinted in thought. 'Indian summer. But we'll be complaining plenty when the cold weather comes.'

Karen hurried inside. She had planned to work on a display corner at the front of the shop that morning.

'Karen, you're always so early,' Sophie scolded. 'Better you should sleep a little later.'

'I've always felt guilty when I've slept past seven,' Karen confessed. 'As though I was reneging on something I should be doing.'

'We haven't heard a word from Joe.' Sophie answered Karen's unspoken question. 'I'm so scared for him.'

'He'll discover there's no way he can get to Afghanistan.' Karen forced an air of optimism. 'And then he'll come home.'

'I pray for that.' Sophie's face was anguished. 'I live for my boys.'

The phone rang. Karen went to respond.

'Good morning, The Oasis.'

'May I speak to Sophie, please?' The woman at the other end sounded disconcerted.

'Just a moment.' Karen turned to Sophie who was at her side. 'Should I ask who's calling?'

'I'll take it,' Sophie said indulgently. 'This is my shop – not some big corporation.' Sophie focused on the caller. 'Hello.' She listened for a moment. 'You don't have to apologize – I understand. You were frightened.' She paused again. 'Yes, of course you can come back.' Sophie seemed distressed. 'Yes, today if you like.' She talked a few moments longer, then put down the phone.

'That's your saleswoman ready to return to her job,' Karen interpreted.

'I realize you want to find something more satisfying. More financially rewarding. But I'll miss you.' Sophie was wistful.

'We'll see each other,' Karen promised.

'I want to continue the newsletter,' Sophie said. 'Will you do it for me? For a fee,' she added, almost apologetically.

'I'll do it – it doesn't take long. But not for a fee,' Karen insisted. 'For the experience. We'll do it together.'

She must find herself a steady job, Karen reminded herself. It was scary to realize how fast her cash reserve

105

would go if she wasn't drawing a regular salary. She should have been answering ads these weeks she'd been here at the shop with Sophie.

It had been understood from the first day that if she had an appointment, she could leave the shop for as long as was required. Again, she reproached herself, she'd been hiding her head in the sand. Enough of that.

Fifteen

Doug sat in the courtroom and waited for the grand jury to return its verdict in the case against Cal and Bart Henderson. So the DA was pissed at him for putting up a strong case. How the hell could any self-respecting jury not indict those two?

Meanwhile, he studied the letter he'd written to *The Sentinel* about the need for a civilian patrol. Mike had promised to run it in tomorrow morning's edition. It was clear and concise, he decided, and slid it back into his briefcase.

He glanced at his watch. The jury had been out for over three hours. Not a good sign, he thought uneasily and then sat up straight and alert. The grand jury was returning. He was conscious of a tic in his right eyelid. No way he could fathom what the decision would be.

He felt a surge of relief when heard the verdict. Cal and Bart Henderson were to be held for trial.

'Bail hearing will be held tomorrow morning at 10 a.m.,' the judge decreed.

Doug leapt to his feet. 'Your Honor, I object.'

'Overruled,' the judge announced. 'Bail hearing will be held tomorrow morning at 10 a.m.,' he repeated. With relish, Doug noted. The old bastard wanted them to be released on bail. But they had to be able to post bail, he reminded himself.

Doug left the courtroom with the conviction that while bail might be approved, there was no way the Henderson family – living in a trailer park with a spasmodic income –

Julie Ellis

would be able to meet it. With no cash assets, no property to put up as collateral for bail, Cal and Bart would remain in jail.

He hurried to *The Sentinel* office to deliver his Letter to the Editor to Mike. He chatted for a moment with the receptionist, and was then ushered into Mike's cluttered office that always appeared as though a hurricane had blown through.

'I've talked to the guys on staff,' Mike reported, seated behind his desk and swinging back and forth in his worse-for-wear chair. Not a good sign. Mike's secretary said the velocity with which he swung in his desk chair was a barometer for what he was about to say. 'Two – including me – will be available for your civilian patrol.'

'That's a start. We've got three of us right now.' He refused to consider that the manpower might be unavailable.

'What happened with the grand jury?' Mike leaned forward, his eyes searching Doug's.

'We got lucky. They're being held for trial. The bail hearing is tomorrow at 10 a.m. I opposed it, of course. But I was overruled. There's not much chance they'll be able to post it.'

'Don't count on that,' Mike warned and Doug lifted his eyebrows in surprise. 'Too many people in this town think with him. Some asshole might bail them out.'

Doug shrugged this off. 'So they'll get out on bail. I'm going to fight like hell for a conviction.' But, in truth, he found it hard to believe that anybody in town would put up bail for two such creeps. They would feel no compunction about leaving anyone who posted bail in the lurch.

Arriving at his office this morning, Doug was greeted by Olivia with the report that the DA had called three times.

'He wants to chew me out about putting up a battle at the grand jury hearing,' Doug interpreted. 'His term as district attorney may be his last.'

108

'You're due at the bail hearing in twenty minutes,' Olivia reminded him.

'I'm leaving in a few minutes,' he soothed. 'Any word from the Sunshine syndicate? Not a peep,' he added before she could reply. 'They're hanging on for Fredericks' re-election. And that ain't going to happen,' he said with fervor.

He left the office, hurried to the bail hearing. The hearing room was almost deserted. Only Cal and Bart's father sat on a front bench. Doug took his position as prosecuting attorney.

The judge took his place, surveyed the meager attendance. Cal and Bart's attorney rose to present his case – the same routine he'd offered at the grand jury hearing.

'I'm aware of the mitigating circumstances,' the judge said. So, what happened in New York and Washington and Pennsylvania gave them the right to beat up an innocent citizen – just because he was of Arab descent? Doug thought cynically. 'And the two defendants have no record of any previous criminal offenses. Therefore, the granting of bail is indicated.'

Doug leapt to feet. 'Your Honor, I object to this flagrant—'

'Objection overruled,' the judge said brusquely. 'Bail is set at five thousand dollars for each of the defendants.'

With an air of triumph Jud Henderson stood up. He held up a check. *A blank check? They couldn't have known what the figure would be. Or could they? What the hell is going on?*

'We're prepared to meet bail, Your Honor.'

Fighting frustration, Karen left the appliance store where she had just applied for a job as cashier. The manager's voice echoed in her head.

'Miss Hunter, I don't think you would be happy in this position considering your background. But I do wish you the best of luck.'

109

She returned to her car and sat motionless behind the wheel. This was the third turndown she'd encountered this morning. Because of her salary record? She understood that salaries were considerably lower out of the major cities. And how many small businesses needed the kind of marketing expertise she'd provided in her last eighteen months of work?

She checked her watch. It was close to 3 p.m. The only other job listed into today's *Star* instructed applicants to apply before 2 p.m. OK, tackle that one tomorrow. Yet instinct warned her that a supermarket manager interviewing for positions as cashiers – paying $7 an hour – would take one look at her resumé and say 'no thanks.' And the super-market wasn't even open yet – that date vague.

All right, focus on re-doing the resumé tonight. Just list all those low-paying, dull jobs she'd held before joining the company at the World Trade Center. Fabricate some-thing unimpressive for the last three years. Some small firm at the Twin Towers that was now out of business since the attack.

She'd started at the company in a low-paying job, moved up fast. *Why can't I do that again?* Willing herself to be optimistic about the future, she headed for home. She felt a sense of nostalgia as she approached the elementary school she'd attended years ago. The building had been enlarged since those days, refurbished.

School was out. She smiled at the hordes of students pouring down the streets. She slowed down to the required speed as she passed the school. And then, a block beyond, she stiffened in attention. What were those little boys doing to the little girl in the center?

'Arab, Arab! Murderer!'

'Why don't you go back where you came from, Arab?'

In shock – while the little girl flailed out ineffectually, in tears now – Karen pulled to a stop, thrust open the car door and darted across the street.

'Stop it, you kids!' she yelled at the taunting boys – no more than ten years old, she judged. 'Stop it!' She struggled to brush them aside, but they were ignoring her efforts.

'Knock it off!' a man's voice ordered. A familiar voice, she realized subconsciously. 'OK, beat it! Go home! Get out of here!'

Karen reached to draw the sobbing little girl into her arms – all at once conscious that the man who'd driven off the little monsters was Doug.

'Karen.' His voice was a startled whisper.

'I'll take her home.' Her own voice was uneven. 'Darling, it's all right,' she said gently. 'You're all right now.' But was she, after hearing those awful taunts?

'Karen, it's great to see you.'

'Thanks for coming to our rescue . . .' She focused her gaze on the little girl. 'I'll take her home now.'

'You – you're staying here in town?' Doug asked. He'd asked her that the last time they met.

'Most likely. Yes,' she added more forcefully.

'Karen, I want to see you again.'

'I think not.' She reached into her purse for a tissue, made an effort to wipe away the little girl's tears. 'It's all right, darling,' she soothed. 'Those monsters have gone away. I'll take you home.'

'I'm not a murderer . . .'

'Of course you're not,' Karen insisted. 'What's your name?'

'Beth.'

'All right, Beth, I'll drive you home. Those were very bad boys. I'm going to call the school and tell the principal what happened. And it won't happen again.'

'You're sure?' Karen saw the doubt in Beth's tear-filled eyes, along with a plaintive hope that this could be true.

'I'm sure.' Karen offered a confident smile. 'You know, a long time ago I went to that same school.'

Beth looked at her with wonder. 'You did?'

'So did I,' Doug added gently. 'A long time ago.'

'Thanks for your help.' Karen reached for Beth's hand and avoided Doug's eyes. 'I'll take her home,' she repeated.

'Karen, we need to talk . . .' For an instant his eyes held hers and telegraphed an urgent message.

For a tumultuous moment Karen hesitated. This was the Doug she'd known long ago. Warm and caring. But that was one Doug. She'd met the other, who'd walked out of her life, leaving her devastated. She battled for calm.

'I think not,' she said with a detachment that belied her inner turmoil. 'We did that a long time ago.'

Sixteen

With Beth's hand in hers, Karen walked with her across the street to her car.

'My house is just two blocks down the street,' Beth told her. 'I–I could walk.' But Karen saw terror lingering in her eyes.

'I'll drive you.' Karen squeezed Beth's hand in a gesture of affection. 'And I'll walk you to the door.' The five little boys hadn't arrived at their feelings about Arab-Americans on their own, she thought, with a fresh stirring of rage. They'd heard those feelings expressed at home. That was wrong!

'Why did they say those awful things?' Beth lifted her face in plaintive inquiry as Karen drove into the stream of light traffic.

'Because they're very stupid – and bad.' She felt a rush of remorse – reproach – that she had also harbored fears about Arab-Americans. *How could I have condemned a whole class of people because of what happened at the World Trade Center – and at the Pentagon and on that plane in Pennsylvania?*

'My mom walks with me to school and back home again, but she couldn't this morning. She's got a bad cold.' Beth hesitated. 'She never used to walk me to school . . .' Her voice trailed off. Because until this insanity arrived, no child had to worry about being attacked, Karen concluded.

'Some – some evil people did terrible acts in this country.

113

And this caused a lot of fear.' Karen sought for words that would reach out to a ten-year-old girl. 'And when people are afraid, sometimes they don't think clearly – they do stupid things. But most people are good, Beth – and this ugliness will go away.'

'I wish people didn't do bad things.' All at once Beth was angry. 'They make my mom cry.'

'Tell me when we reach your house,' Karen said with an encouraging smile, and Beth nodded.

A few minutes later Karen parked before a modest frame-house with pots of 'mums alternating with coleus on the stairs leading to the porch. She walked with Beth to the door and waited for her mother to appear. With a sympathetic smile Karen explained what had happened.

'I should have been there to walk her home,' Beth's mother chastised herself, shaken by what had happened. 'I know what it's been like since – since . . .' She avoided completing the sentence. 'How do we make people understand that Islam is a peaceful religion? We don't hate anyone.' She struggled for composure, managed a shaky smile. 'Thank you for bringing Beth home.' She reached out with an air of urgency to bring her small daughter close.

'I'll call the school and tell the principal what happened,' Karen promised. 'It's outrageous that Beth was subjected to such ugliness.'

Back behind the wheel of her car Karen unwarily recalled the tense encounter with Doug. No room in her life for him. No room in her life for any man – now that she'd lost Greg.

Recoiling from the prospective encounter she circled around to drive back to the school. She must let the principal know what had happened to one of his vulnerable young students. Belatedly, she realized she didn't know Beth's surname. But it would be enough to report what had happened.

*   *   *

Doug sat across the desk from Mike and in colorful language offered his reaction to what had happened to a small, defenseless little girl here in their own town.

'Damn it, Mike! How can something so rotten happen in a decent small town like ours?'

'How did it happen that Marty Mohammed was beaten to a pulp?' Mike slammed a fist on his desk, swung about in his chair in a gesture of frustration. 'How did it happen that the pizza store on Main Street was torched – and that fire at the produce store? People have gone berserk. And it's not just in this town,' he admitted. 'It's happening in other towns across the country.'

'And *The Star* keeps writing inflammatory editorials about how we have to guard against the "foreigners in our midst" – making it clear they're referring to local Arab-Americans. These are American citizens – some here for decades, some born here – who work hard for a living, pay taxes, vote.' Doug churned with frustration. 'Mike, you have to fight this.'

'Hell, what do you call my editorials?' Mike challenged.

'I know.' Doug managed a lopsided smile. 'I just get so pissed that this can be happening in Weston. It must have been like this in the McCarthy period.'

Mike nodded grimly. 'And in the civil rights battles and in the internment of West Coast Japanese-Americans during World War Two. We never seem to learn.' He shook his head in disgust. 'And by the way – where the hell did the Henderson jerks's father get the loot to bail them out? They have trouble coming up with enough to buy a bucket of KFC.'

'Yeah,' Doug said. 'It hit me, too. Somebody in this town put up the bail money – but why?'

'It smells bad, Doug. Was that the pay-off for their beating up Marty Mohammed?' Mike squinted in thought. 'Could this have political overtones?'

'You suspect somebody set him up?'

115

'These days I suspect things too rotten to mention,' Mike confessed. 'So I'm wrong.' He shrugged. 'I hate what's happening to our town. It used to be a good place to live.'

'I hate the way *The Star* keeps crying over the two "innocent guys" being persecuted by the District Attorney's office. Nobody in the office wanted to take the case except me,' Doug admitted.

'I know the crap they throw.' Mike grimaced. 'How you have no case all. No witnesses, only Marty Mohammed's statement that he was attacked. "It was late at night – no moonlight. How could he see who came up behind him?"' Mike mimicked contemptuously.

'Marty's a responsible citizen. He's a college graduate, going on to architectural school. Those two hoodlums are high-school dropouts, no steady jobs.' But Doug knew he had a tough case. 'Mike.' Doug paused, his mind charging ahead. 'I'm writing a Letter to the Editor about what happened today. Will you run it?'

'Sit down at my computer and knock it out right now,' Mike ordered. 'It'll appear on the first page of tomorrow morning's *Sentinel*.'

An hour later – the letter written – Doug emerged from *The Sentinel* building and headed for his own office. He still had a practice to handle, he derided himself. Finish off the day's work, head for campaign headquarters and a lengthy conference with Tony and the inner circle. It was early yet, he reminded himself – but the polls were too close for comfort.

Only now did he allow himself to consider that unexpected encounter with Karen. It had been festering within him since the moment he saw her rushing to that little girl's aid. A typical Karen gesture, he thought tenderly.

Seeing Karen, he felt as though the past ten years had evaporated. She'd lingered in a corner of his mind since the moment he'd run into her in Sophie's shop. He ached to hold her in his arms again, to tell her what a stupid ass he'd been. Make her understand there could be a second chance for them.

But in all this craziness what chance do I have with her?

After a nightmare-haunted slumber, Karen awoke to a gray, cool morning. She stalled on rising, pulled the light coverlet above her shoulders. She should have worked on a new resumé last night, she reproached herself. She was conscious of how her funds diminished each week. Even a low-paying job seemed elusive, she thought in simmering alarm.

She was here. She couldn't bring herself to move back to New York. She mustn't allow herself to be intimidated by Doug's presence. This was her home. Her roots.

Reluctantly she left her bed, reached for her robe, hurried – shivering – into the bathroom. Turn on the hot water, steam up the room before showering. She stood there waiting for comforting warmth to invade the small room.

Her mind shot back to the scene near the elementary school yesterday. *How could I have allowed myself to be afraid of anyone of Arab background because of what happened on September 11th? I'd been traumatized. I hadn't thought clearly.*

She flinched, recalling articles she'd read in current national magazines about others who were reacting with hatred towards innocent people who happened to be of Arab extraction. Lisa had tried to make her understand. But not until she'd seen tiny, terrified Beth being attacked by those little boys had she understood what Lisa had been trying to tell her.

The room was steamy now. *All right, shower, prepare for the day. Pick up* The Star – *because* The Sentinel *carried a meager amount of Help Wanted ads. Be aggressive. I must find a job – no matter how low the pay. I can't let my reserve keep dropping.*

Scolding herself for this extravagance, Karen headed for the Main Street Diner for breakfast. She'd pick up *The Star*, read the classified ads while she ate, then follow whatever leads there were. But driving towards her destination her mind darted back to the encounter yesterday afternoon.

She'd been unnerved to discover Doug charging towards that ugly scene along with her. It was the kind of thing she'd expect of the Doug she thought she knew. And for one agonizing moment she'd thought, yes, let's talk. Let him make me understand why he put me through such hell.

Now she focused on finding a parking spot close to the diner. There, she thought with relief and headed to claim it. The newspaper store was two doors from the diner. From habit she picked up just *The Star*, then froze as her eyes scanned the front page of *The Sentinel*.

Paying for the two newspapers, she hurriedly read the Letter to the Editor placed in the center of the front page. A letter from Doug about what had happened yesterday afternoon to sweet little Beth – just a block away from the elementary school. Her heart pounding, she walked into the diner, found an empty small booth towards the rear.

Carefully she re-read the letter. *The Sentinel* condemned what was happening to Arab-Americans – not only in their town but across America. Now she recalled that Lisa had said that *The Sentinel*'s publisher and editor – supporting the effort to vote out the corrupt Fredericks administration – was fighting for survival. It was a fine gesture, she thought with admiration, for the editor to have run that letter on the front page of this morning's *Sentinel*.

'Good morning.' An ebullient waitress arrived to take her order. 'It's a great day out there.' Clouds had given way to sun.

'Right.' Karen managed a smile. Great for some people. Not for all the people around the world who were horrified at the terrorism that threatened to erupt at any time – in any area.

The world had changed on September 11th. But the terrorists mustn't be allowed to rule. What was happening here in Weston – to Beth and to Sophie's son and to the owners of the pizza store and the produce shop – must be stopped. She reached for *The Sentinel*, and re-read Doug's letter again.

Maybe it's a stupid thing to do – but I want to write another letter, re-enforcing what Doug's said. We must make people understand what a horrible act they're perpetrating when they attack innocent people for no reason other than their ethnic heritage. I'm furious at what's happening.

Seventeen

Doug had arrived early at his office that morning – an hour before Olivia was due to arrive. He'd awakened before 6 a.m., tried without success to return to sleep. Now he stifled a series of yawns. For one precious moment yesterday afternoon he'd felt a tumultuous contact with Karen. She had not forgotten what it had been like for them back in the old days, he'd told himself joyously. But then the moment splintered.

He sat down at his desk, reached for *The Sentinel* he'd picked up on his way in. True to his word, Mike had slapped the letter right on the front page. And as per his own instructions last evening, photocopies of the letter would be circulated by Mendoza volunteers later today.

The phone rang. He lifted an eyebrow. A call so early? He picked up. 'Doug Madison, good morning.'

'Doug, it's me, Sophie.' Her voice was anxious. 'I tried you at home – you were gone. I figured you'd be at the office. It's Marty now. He read somewhere that the government's anxious to hire Arabic interpreters. He wants to go down to Washington to volunteer. He can't do that, can he? I mean, isn't he needed as a witness at the trial?'

'Absolutely. Without him to testify we have no case.' *Marty mustn't leave Sophie alone in that house at the edge of town. I get bad vibes at the thought. And where the hell is Joe?*

'Will you talk to him?' Sophie was fighting for calm.

'Is he at the same construction site?'

'Yes,' Sophie said. 'I understand he wants to be useful – and the government needs these interpreters desperately. But he has to be here for the trial.' She paused. 'Or could he accept a job with the provision that he can return for the trial?'

'He could. But I want him here with you at this time,' Doug said bluntly. 'I don't want you alone at the house. I'll talk to Marty – make him understand.'

'Is it wrong of me to try to keep him here?' There was a plaintive note in Sophie's voice now.

'He needs to be here. I'll make him understand,' Doug promised.

In her apartment Karen sat before her computer and wrote – and revised three times – an impassioned letter to *The Sentinel*. Now she re-read it. *It's awfully long – but what I'm saying is necessary.*

She'd reported her own experiences at the World Trade Center, then wrote about the loss of a very dear friend. In truth, Greg had been her best friend in the world in those last three years. She talked about how fate had kept her safe while her friend and colleagues died – and how she had been afraid of anyone whom she encountered who appeared to be of Arab descent.

'This was so wrong,' she wrote. 'But I didn't understand then – I was too traumatized. Then I came home – because Weston is my home. I worked as a temporary sales clerk in Sophie Mohammed's shop, The Oasis – and I told myself, Sophie was special. I still didn't understand how wrong it was to be fearful of people because of their ethnic descent. And then I saw a sweet, innocent little girl attacked by five little boys because she happened to be an Arab-American.'

She continued writing, seeking to build up those moments

when she – and Doug – had rushed to the aid of a terrified little ten-year-old child. And at last – with her third cup of coffee – she agreed this was her best effort.

She sought for an envelope, a stamp, then hesitated. No, don't mail it. Take it over to the newspaper. Hopefully – if the editor accepts it – he'll run the letter in tomorrow morning's paper. It was important to follow up Doug's letter for the most impact.

Feeling a rush of satisfaction, she left the apartment and headed for *The Sentinel*'s office.

Mike Canfield settled down at his desk. A small pile of Letters to the Editor lay in a heap before him. His last task of the day. He regarded them with indulgence. There were the crackpots, yes – but mainly these were people concerned for their town. He gave them a voice.

He leaned back in his chair, sipped at his coffee. There'd be a shitload of letters tomorrow, he surmised. Doug's letter on the front page would guarantee that. And his editorial about setting up a civilian patrol would bring in letters and – hopefully – volunteers for the patrol.

He glanced at his watch. Close to 8 p.m. Go through the letters and get out of here. He began the nightly ritual. The first was an anonymous letter. Damn, they knew the rules. No letter would be run without the writer supplying name, address and phone number. But now and then there was a rush of hate mail – with no names.

Methodically he went through the evening's batch. The last letter, he noted, bore no postage – must have been delivered by hand. Somebody hot under the collar, he surmised. He glanced at the signature: Karen Hunter. Not a name familiar to him. OK, read.

He rushed through the letter with a growing excitement. She'd worked temporarily for Sophie Mohammed – did that mean she was job hunting? He could use an addition to the staff who could write with this kind of passion. He couldn't pay a high salary – but then Sophie couldn't have been paying her much.

He debated for a moment, then reached for the phone. It was picked up on the second ring.

'Hello.'

'May I speak to Karen Hunter, please.'

'This is Karen.' He sensed a kind of wariness.

'I'm Mike Canfield at *The Sentinel*. I've just read your letter. Damn good. It says what people in this town need to hear. It goes on the front page of tomorrow's edition.'

'Thank you, Mr Canfield.'

'Mike,' he said brusquely. 'I gather you're unemployed at the moment?'

'Yes.' An element of astonishment blending with hope in her voice, he interpreted.

'Ever work on a newspaper?' he asked.

'Only on my college newspaper. But I wrote sales letters, market research articles for the past three years. Until the attack at the World Trade Center.'

'I can't offer a fancy salary,' he warned. 'And the job here will include some routine office duties in addition to writing.' He hesitated, raised his initial figure by fifty a week. 'Interested?'

'Yes,' she said instantly.

'OK. Be here at my office tomorrow morning at nine – and I warn you, we don't follow the nine to five routine.'

'No problem,' she said, a lilt in her voice. 'See you tomorrow morning – 9 a.m. sharp.'

Karen sat immobile, staring into space. She had a job on *The Sentinel*. On a newspaper! Sure, the salary was shockingly low after what she'd been earning in New York – but living expenses were lower here. She could manage on what Mike Canfield was willing to pay. *I'll budget. I've done that often enough in the past.*

In a burst of exuberance she reached for the phone to

call Lisa. The answering machine responded. She left a message. She should have known Lisa wouldn't be home. The elections were less than four weeks away. Lisa would be over at the Mendoza campaign headquarters – if not holding some client's hand.

On impulse – eager to share her news – she phoned Sophie, told her that she'd just been hired to work at *The Sentinel*.

'Oh, Karen, I'm so pleased for you. And I have some news, too.' Karen heard the undercurrent of relief in her voice. 'Just a few minutes ago I had a phone call from Joe. I hadn't heard a word in six days. I've been so worried – scared.'

'Where is he?' Karen asked.

'He's down in New York. Doug said he'd never be able to get out of this country. He's coming home in the morning. But I know he's still terribly upset.'

'The situation here is going to change, Sophie. Joe will understand that people acted without thinking because of the horror of what happened.' *Will it change? Can* The Sentinel *wake up this town to what it's creating?*

'I read Doug's letter in this morning's *Sentinel*,' Sophie said tenderly. 'It was wonderful.'

'Yes, it was.' In a way, Karen realized, Doug's letter had brought about her job with the newspaper.

'He's so good for this town. He's setting up a civilian patrol – to make sure there are no more nasty incidents against Arab-Americans in town. Marty told me about it.' Unexpectedly Sophie chuckled. 'Marty said he wants to be part of the patrol. He said to me, 'I'm an American who happens to be of Arab descent. Why can't I be a member of Doug's civilian patrol?'

In the book-cluttered living room of his second-floor garden apartment, Mike Canfield sprawled on his much-worn sofa and – like millions of Americans across the country – watched the 11 p.m. TV news.

A New Day Dawning

Why do I always watch the late news? I already know most of it – and it's almost always bad. How the hell could anybody watch the news and have a decent night's sleep?

He watched – but his mind wandered at regular intervals. He'd been publishing a newspaper in this town for just seven years – and he was still fighting to keep his head above water. He'd worked through the years on a series of lackluster city newspapers that had a way of going down the drain. As long as he could remember – dating back to journalism school – he'd been fretting for a newspaper of his own. And now he had it – thanks to the money he'd inherited when his mother and father died within a year of each other.

The circulation was picking up. The advertising was still just enough to keep the newspaper afloat. Damn it, he was pushing fifty – he ought to be thinking ahead. He chuckled. He wasn't worrying about retiring in fifteen years. If he held on to the paper, they'd probably carry him out feet first.

He'd settled down here – after spending most of his life in midwestern cities – on what Mom would have called a whim. He was tired of the noises and the fast pace of cities – and he remembered all the stories Mom had spun about her growing-up years in Weston, New York. So he'd come and set up *The Sentinel*.

He glowered at the sudden intrusion of the phone. Some new crisis at the paper? He crossed the room to pick up the phone. 'Yeah?'

'You don't sound in the best of moods,' Doug greeted him.

'I thought you were somebody from the paper – that I'd have to go chasing over to clear up some problem. How're you doing?'

'I've just come home from campaign headquarters. But a couple of kids wandered in tonight and asked to speak to me. Not about the campaign,' Doug pinpointed. 'They have a personal grudge against the two Henderson creeps. They

125

were nervous about telling tales, but something happened tonight that pissed them off. They gave me some good leads to follow up. Cal and Bart are not into drugs themselves – at least, they don't think so. But Cal has been pushing pot at the junior high school. I've got somebody tailing him.'

Mike whistled softly. 'And the DA's office is springing for that?'

Doug mustered a sheepish smile. 'I have an office emergency fund. And this isn't some high-powered guy charging three hundred a day. I can handle it.'

'If you need some newspaper follow-up about pot at the junior high school, just say the word.'

'I expect we'll have Cal nabbed damn fast. I have a strong hunch Cal and Bart aren't walking away from the Mohammed trial. They'll face prison time for the assault – plus the drug-selling charge.'

'I can't print it.' Mike sighed regretfully. 'At least, not yet . . .'

'Not yet,' Doug conceded. 'But you will.'

'The DA won't be happy,' Mike warned.

'With a little luck he'll be out of a job on election day. And that's just a bit over three weeks away.'

'What's doing with the supermarket situation?' Mike asked. 'The way it looks, they could open up tomorrow if they had their parking area set.'

'The whole deal's on hold. Since they can't buy at their price, they figure on sitting it out until after the election. Hank Fredericks won't do anything that might cost him votes now – but if he's re-elected, they figure he'll condemn the property and see to it they get it at their price. And he'll get his cut.'

Mike snapped his fingers. 'I've got a bit of news for you. You know your letter in this morning's edition?'

'You've had bomb threats?'

'Not yet – but nothing will surprise me. But you know that gal that you mentioned as going to the rescue of that little ten-year-old? I gather the two of you didn't have time in that brief encounter to exchange names?'

'Her name's Karen Hunter. What about her?' Why does Doug sound suddenly so tense? Mike wondered.

'She sent in a terrific letter. It goes on the front page of tomorrow's edition.' Mike chuckled. 'You two would make a great team.'

'I'll look for the letter in the morning's paper.'

'I called her up, offered her a job on the paper. And she accepted,' Mike said with relish. 'Now don't tell me she's a homely broad. I enjoy having something nice to look at around the office.'

'She's beautiful.' Doug's voice was strained. 'And very bright. You'll enjoy having her around.'

Eighteen

Doug prowled about his small apartment – knowing he was too uptight to sleep. Mike's words ricocheted in his brain: *'You two would make a great team.'* But how was he to convince Karen of that? She wouldn't even let him talk with her!

Still, she'd read his letter and added her own. He clutched at this. Mike said her letter was terrific – it would get the same front-page treatment as his own.

Karen and he still thought alike – felt alike, he told himself with a surge of jubilance. After all these years – when he'd convinced himself he'd at last put the past to rest – Karen came out of nowhere and nothing had changed. He felt the same as he did in those great months they'd shared. As though with Karen at his side he could accomplish anything he wished.

I'd been so sure I'd lost her forever – and here she is, right here in Weston. That's fate telling me we can be together again. It's up to me to convince Karen of that. I have to find a way.

He searched his brain for the proper approach, stalked about the apartment until past midnight, then reluctantly ordered himself to sleep. Tomorrow was another day. There must be a way to make Karen listen to him. To make her understand the insanity that had overtaken him those last days at college.

He tossed about in bed, staring at the ceiling. Searching

his mind. He'd been so damn naive, raised to face his responsibilities. How could he have known he was being played for a prime sucker?

Mom had been dubious about the whole situation. He'd told himself she just didn't want to believe he could have got himself into such a position. But Mom and Dad had always been there for him.

At last he drifted off into troubled sleep. From habit he awoke as usual at 7:30 a.m. He lay against his pillow – reliving each of his three unexpected encounters with Karen. How was he to make his way back into her life? This was the second chance he'd thought would never be.

All at once he felt a surge of excitement. His mind darted back through the years to her 21st birthday. Each day – for 20 days before her birthday and then on her birthday – he'd left a single red rose at her door. She'd kept every rose, dried them and kept them in a vase beside her bed. *That's my way to tell her how I feel.*

Where does she live? How can I find out? She won't be in the current phone directory. The first time I saw her, she was coming out of Amy Lansing's house. Everybody knows Amy rents out an illegal apartment in her house – and everybody looks the other way. Is Amy Karen's landlady?

He reached for the phone on his night table, stopped himself. He couldn't call Amy at this hour of the morning – or could he? Amy always said she was awake at 6 a.m. and 'ready for action.' More than once she was at campaign headquarters by 7 a.m. when they had a rush mailing to get out. She even had a key. Call her.

He punched in Amy's number.

'Good morning,' Amy chirped. 'Remember election is just twenty-five days away. Vote for Tony Mendoza and his slate!'

'We're winning that election,' Doug predicted. 'It's about time. I hope I'm not calling you too early?'

'Doug, you know better than that,' Amy chided. 'What's on your mind?'

'I wasn't sure that you'd rented out your – guest room,' he began. 'I know someone who might be looking for one soon.'

'Oh, yeah.' Amy chuckled. 'Got myself a darling tenant.'

'Anybody I know?'

'I doubt it. She's just moved into town after being away for years.' *Karen.* 'But if you're smart, you'll get to know her. She's a honey.'

'I might just try that.' Doug tried for a flip tone. 'Will you expect a fee if something comes of it?'

'For you, Doug, it's on the house.'

Doug rushed through the morning routine – anxious to be out of the house and reading Karen's Letter to the Editor. This would be one of those mornings he'd have breakfast at the Main Street Diner. It was going to be a hectic day.

He had an early conference with Tony at campaign head-quarters. At around 1 p.m. he was to hear from the guy tailing Cal Henderson – not that he was sure Cal would be peddling drugs at the school lunch hour, but he was hoping – and he'd put in a call to the fancy New York lawyer representing the Sunshine people.

He bought the morning's edition of *The Sentinel* at the news-stand next door to the diner, stood there and read Karen's letter. What a sharp brain she had, he thought with pride. She'd hit all bases. A stronger letter than his own – strong because it was sharing her own troubled feelings – admitting she'd been wrong in her thinking and changing that. Not just a letter – an article.

Now he abandoned the prospect of immediate breakfast. He had a red rose to buy and deliver. Then he would have breakfast, make notes about what had to be accomplished today. But most important of all – he told himself – he must lay that red rose at Karen's door.

* * *

Karen awoke with instant realization that she was going to a job this morning. Her heart began to pound. She felt a blend of anticipation and a simmering alarm. For an anguished moment her mind shot back through the weeks to the day Greg had insisted she not go in to work. No, don't think about that now.

What should she wear? One of her summer pantsuits – that was standard in offices everywhere. She should have shampooed her hair last night – it was too late now. Oh, stop thinking about such stupid trivialities. She was going to work at *The Sentinel*. She wasn't entering a contest for Miss Congeniality.

Not until she stood beneath a stinging hot shower did she admit to herself that she felt a tug of inadequacy. Was she ready for this job? She didn't even know what was required of her. Mike Canfield had no idea of her capabilities. Was he expecting more than she had to offer? The old insecurities threatened to inundate her.

Was she getting in beyond her depth? Had Mike Canfield been carried away by the emotions of her letter? Don't think that way, she ordered herself. And now Greg's words to her on other such occasions filtered across her mind: '*Karen, you can do this. Just keep saying to yourself, "I can handle this. I'm not a scared little girl. I'm a woman – with a future. I can handle whatever challenges me."*'

In a sudden need to talk to Lisa, to tell her about the job, she left the shower, hurriedly dressed. She debated about having breakfast, then calling Lisa – or vice versa. Call her now, she decided. So it was early, Lisa wouldn't mind.

'Hello.' Lisa's effervescent voice came to her.

'Lisa, I have a job. Starting this morning.'

'Great! Tell me about it,' Lisa ordered.

Words tumbling over one another in her excitement, Karen described her encounter with Mike Canfield.

'Of course, I'm scared to death he hired me on the spur of the moment,' Karen admitted. 'I mean, he's all revved up over this business of the local anti-Arab feeling in town.'

'Mike's sharp. He wouldn't have hired you if he wasn't damn sure you were right for the job. And I'm dying to read your letter in *The Sentinel.*'

'I feel so ashamed of my attitude, Lisa.'

'You were in shock. You've come out of it. I'm busy as hell now with the election – I go straight to campaign head-quarters from the office every day. But why don't we grab a quick dinner at the diner tonight? You'll understand that I can't hang around to yak.'

'Great.' Now Karen hesitated, in doubt. 'I don't know what time I'll be able to get away.'

'I'll call you when I'm about to leave the office, check with you,' Lisa soothed. 'Mike Canfield's a great guy – he won't keep you late on your first day on the job.'

Determined not to be a moment late, Karen prepared to leave her apartment far earlier than necessary. No need to buy this morning's newspaper, she told herself with a touch of whimsy. She was on staff – though, in truth, not yet sure of what her duties would be.

She reached into her purse for keys, pulled the door wide. She gazed in surprise at the perfect red rose that lay at her feet. Ten years seemed to disappear for one moment as she remembered the single red rose Doug had left at her door each morning of the 20 days leading up to her 21st birthday.

A tightening in her throat, she stood frozen for another moment. It was a mistake. Somebody had meant to leave the rose for Amy. She bent to pick it up, walked around the porch that led to Amy's front door.

Her hand trembling, she placed the single red rose there and hurried away.

*   *   *

Swigging down his second cup of coffee at the Main Street Diner, Doug re-read – for the fourth time – Karen's Letter to the Editor. He was touched that she could bring herself to admit to the world at large that she, too, had been guilty of intolerance. Somewhere along the way, he thought with a rush of tenderness, she had learned to overcome her painful insecurities. But did that bode well for him?

He glanced at his watch. OK, run over to campaign headquarters for his 8 a.m. meeting with Tony. God, the days were racing past! Two months ago he was sure their slate would clobber the Fredericks crowd. Now he was apprehensive – despite his show of optimism.

Who would have suspected that what happened on September 11th down in Manhattan would affect even a local election in Weston? Hank Fredericks and his crew were playing dirty – preying on the insane fears of some voters' terror. Sufficient voters, he warned himself, to swing the election in Fredericks' favor.

Striding down Main Street to the storefront headquarters of their campaign, Doug saw Tony at the door – key in hand.

'Hi,' Doug called. 'Did you see this morning's *Sentinel*?'

'Bless Mike.' Tony pantomimed his gratitude. 'He's still fighting for us. But you don't want to see *The Star*,' he warned, throwing the door wide. 'They saw your letter yesterday and went into full battle mode this morning. "This town needs Hank Fredericks to protect it from foreign terrorists."' Tony mimicked. '"America for Americans."'

Inside, they strode to Tony's office at the rear, settled themselves in chairs flanking the small conference table that dominated the room. For at least half an hour they'd be alone here, Doug reminded himself. Precious 'plotting time.' Let them focus on strategy to reach more voters – on a tight budget.

'I got a call late last night – after we talked,' Tony reported, a vein hammering in his forehead.

Tony's scared we're too short on money. We've already

been far outspent by the opposition. If we lose, it won't be the first bought election.

Tony continued. 'It's leaked out that the Fredericks mob is getting a huge contribution for a last-minute blitz from some out-of-town corporation. Somebody with an axe to grind.'

'The Sunshine Supermarket,' Doug pounced. 'They want Fredericks in as mayor so they can get their parking lot set.'

'How the hell did they go this far without buying the acres they needed?' Tony slammed a fist on the conference table in frustration.

'Tony, you know,' Doug scolded. 'Property prices went soaring when word broke that Sunshine was opening up in town. Every small property owner had visions of a bonanza. Fredericks told Sunshine to cool it when they'd bought the acreage for the store. He promised to make sure they got the parking-lot space at their own price.'

'We don't actually know that . . .' But Tony sounded convinced.

'We've pieced it together these past months. That's the way it had to be. And I'll take any bets that this new influx of campaign funds is coming straight from Sunshine. They know if you move into the mayor's office, you won't play footsie with them.'

'What's happening with your deal with them?' Tony stirred restlessly.

'They know what my people will accept. They're hoping for a much lower purchase price.' Doug grimaced in rejection. 'So they're stalling on further negotiations until after the election.'

'They're creating bad feelings for themselves. They interviewed an army of people for jobs – and now everything's just frozen.'

'They're not losing any money on this delay. They'll write it off on their taxes.'

'So what do we do to make sure that Fredericks doesn't win another term?' Tony challenged. 'Hey, you're supposed to be the brains on this team.'

Nineteen

Karen waited for the printer to spit out the article she'd just completed for Mike Canfield's approval. She glanced at her watch. A few minutes past 6 p.m. Mike had said this wasn't a 9 to 5 job – but then her hours at her last company had often stretched well past 5 p.m.

Lisa hadn't called. That meant she was running late, too. Talk to Mike, then call Lisa to see if even their 'quick dinner' was off. She reached for the printed-out pages – conscious that she was tired and tense, yet also exhilarated. She'd survived her first day on the job – thus far – with no problems. All right, take this article to Mike.

She paused tentatively at the open door to Mike's office.

'Don't stand there – come in,' Mike ordered. A hand extended for the article. He'd warned her that Dr Kendricks, the principal of the elementary school, could be brusque with reporters from *The Sentinel*: '*Kendricks is so far right he makes Pat Robertson look like a liberal.*' All at once Mike grinned. 'The old bastard give you a rough time?'

'He was wary,' Karen conceded. 'Full of fancy talk about how his student body came from good families. He dismissed the incident with that sweet little Beth as an aberration.'

'Oh sure,' Mike chortled. 'Those five little monsters thought up Arab-hating all on their own. It didn't come from their righteous parents.' Now he began to read, reached for a red pencil. 'You're writing for a newspaper,' he exhorted. 'Keep it tight.' He was silent for a few moments, then lifted his gaze to focus on Karen with an air of disbelief. 'You convinced Kendricks to call an emergency meeting of teachers and parents? You slipped something into his coffee?'

'It was a hard sell,' Karen admitted. 'I finally convinced him his image was at stake.'

'The meeting is scheduled for Monday evening,' Mike noted. 'OK, you be there to do a follow-up article.'

Karen called Lisa's office, discovered Lisa had been about to call her.

'I'll be at the diner in fifteen minutes,' Lisa told her. 'If you're there first, grab a booth for us.'

She'd just settled herself into a booth that afforded some privacy when she spied Lisa coming into the diner at her usual breakneck pace.

'I'm famished,' Lisa said, sliding into their booth and at the same time signaling to a waiter that they were in a hurry.

The waiter rushed over. Karen and Lisa settled for white western omelets and coffee.

'So,' Lisa said with a convivial smile when they were alone again. 'You survived your first day on the job.'

'I spent a lot of time at the copier, then faxing. But the time flew. About 2 p.m. Mike yelled for me. He'd decided to pursue the problem with kids and name-calling, sent me over to the elementary school to interview the principal.' Karen frowned in recall. 'He wasn't there when we were in elementary school.'

'He's been principal about six years.' Lisa grimaced. 'We've had trouble with him on several occasions. He can't believe that his perfect little students can do anything wrong.'

'There's to be an emergency meeting of parents and teachers at seven on Monday evening.' Karen glowed.

'Well!'

'Mike was surprised, too. Oh, he said the polls on the

mayor's race show Tony Mendoza and Fredericks running neck and neck.'

'Ever since 9/11 we've had problems. I never thought that could happen here.' Lisa grunted in exasperation. 'Did you see *The Star* this morning?'

'I don't allow it in my apartment now.'

'It's part of my job with the campaign to read the rag. They're beginning a vendetta against the four property owners who won't sell to the Sunshine people. I know,' she added before Karen could speak. 'The Sunshine people want to buy at fire-sale prices. And, of course,' she drawled with contempt, 'they're blaming Sophie as the ringleader of the group. "Our local Middle-Eastern troublemaker."'

'On my lunch break I heard a group of late teenagers complaining about the supermarket's delay in opening. I gather they all expect to get jobs there.' Entry-level jobs, Karen suspected, at little above minimum wages.

'Tony and Doug have been exploring the job situation for young people. So many leave because all they can find here in town are minimum-wage jobs. Doug has some plan for approaching outside businesses that require skilled workers to come into town. You know, with tax breaks and other goodies.' Lisa's eyes were questioning.

'I'd love to be a volunteer,' Karen said apologetically – reading Lisa's mind. 'But it would mean running into Doug all the time. I–I'm not ready for that.' That single red rose this morning had been unnerving. But it had been left by mistake – it was meant for Amy.

'I'd better eat and get out of here.' Lisa sighed. 'I need more than twenty-four hours a day at this point in my life. But I tell Howie – and part of me believes it – if Hank Fredericks gets elected for another term, I'm ready to move out of town.'

The Mendoza headquarters was running at full throttle. Doug had just proof-read the latest mailing, scheduled to go out the following morning. He couldn't erase from his mind what Tony had told him about a major corporate contribution the Fredericks campaign had just received. That meant, he surmised, another blitz of commercials.

He glanced up and saw Lisa approaching. She was great, the way she busted her butt trying to dig up new donors. But individual donors faded in comparison to the corporate donors.

'Hi,' he greeted her.

'All set for the new mailing?'

'It's OK.' Doug frowned. 'But it needs more passion – more something,' he said impatiently. 'We've all had a hand in it,' he told her, 'but it lacks – pizzazz.'

'I know somebody.' Lisa hesitated. 'She's worked in marketing – and she's very sharp. And she's on our side. Could you hold up on running it for a couple of hours? I could run over and ask her to make suggestions. Maybe an hour?'

'Yeah,' Doug agreed after a moment. 'I don't suppose she'd come over here? We could sit down and thrash this out together.'

'I don't think so.' Lisa's eyes went opaque. 'But I think she could be helpful.'

Who's this marketing whiz that won't come over to headquarters? Doug wondered.

'OK.' Doug shrugged. 'Let me make a copy, then you run with it.'

'We'll get it set, run it tonight. It'll go out first thing in the morning. I'll stay as long as it takes.' Lisa nodded with conviction. 'We'll make it a blockbuster effort.'

Karen was startled at the sound of her doorbell. Who would be coming here? Probably some kid selling cookies or raffle tickets, she guessed, and went to the door.

'We need some help,' Lisa said without preliminaries.

'Who's "we"?' Karen asked, pulling the door wide.

'The Tony Mendoza campaign.' Lisa reached into her

tote as she walked into the apartment. 'We've got this mailing that has to go out tomorrow morning – and it just doesn't sell. Give us a hand?' Lisa cajoled. 'Sophie has been lyrical about the sales letter you did for her – and that was your job for three years.'

'Actually, the last eighteen months on the job,' Karen said with candor. 'I'll put up tea and then look at your mailing.' *Has Lisa said something to Doug about me? Are they playing games?*

'I'll put up the tea,' Lisa said. 'You read.'

Karen settled herself on a corner of the sofa and began to read. 'Shall I make my revisions right on this copy – or do notes?' she asked. 'I don't want to step on toes.'

'Make corrections on the copy,' Lisa called from the kitchenette. 'No ego problem here.'

Karen enmeshed herself in the task at hand. This was good – it just needed some punch here and there. It covered vital issues that the Fredericks people ignored.

Lisa brought mugs of Earl Grey to the coffee table and sipped while Karen worked.

'Drink your tea while it's hot,' Lisa ordered. 'You know, you're not revising the Declaration of Independence.'

'The more I read about the Fredericks administration the more I loathe it.'

'You haven't got time to loathe,' Lisa warned. 'I need to go back to headquarters with that, give it to a volunteer to run off a load of copies, then get the crew to mail out a sizeable chunk. The rest will be hand-distributed around town in the morning.'

'I think this is the best I can do on short notice.' Karen handed over the copy. 'Lisa, I do want to be helpful.'

'You're a doll.' Lisa leaned forward to kiss her lightly on one cheek. 'But Doug was curious about why my "friend" couldn't come over to campaign headquarters and do her thing.'

Karen stiffened. 'This is Doug's copy? You didn't tell him about me?'

'Not a peep,' Lisa soothed. 'I just have a "reclusive best friend."' Let me get back over there. I'd like to be out by a fairly respectable hour tonight. This is one of those nights when Howie claims visiting privileges.'

Doug looked up from his cluttered desk as Lisa strolled into the office he shared with Tony.

'She did it?' His eyes were hopeful.

'For her it was a snap. I think she did a great job.' Lisa handed him the copy, dropped into a chair across from him.

He reached for the copy, began to read. All at once questions leapt into his mind. He recalled Karen's letter in *The Sentinel.*

This is the same style – I can almost hear Karen talking!

'Is your friend who revised this for us—' He took a deep breath. 'Is she Karen Hunter?'

Lisa stared at him in dismay. Karen had told Lisa not to identify her, he realized.

'Did Karen tell you about us?' he asked gently.

Lisa nodded.

'There was a horrible screw-up. All my fault,' Doug said painfully. 'Let me tell you about it.'

In blunt terms – because he knew Lisa would understand – he told her about the ordeal with Candy, his gullibility, the outcome.

'After the divorce I came back here. I'd hoped to find Karen, to be able to explain to her why I ran out like that. To convince her that we could have a great life together. But she hadn't returned to Weston after college graduation. I asked around – nobody seemed to know where she'd gone. I cursed myself for losing her – hurting her. And then one evening last month I came from visiting a client who'd been injured in a car crack-up – and there she was, just across the street. I was too stunned – and scared,' he confessed, 'to approach her.'

'She's been through a rough time. She worked for a

company in the World Trade Center.' Lisa seemed to be searching for words.

'I know,' Doug said gently. 'She talked about that in her letter. She lost a very close friend.' And the Karen he remembered was close to very few people.

'The friend she talked about—' Lisa paused, seeming in inner debate. 'That was Greg – the man she was to marry the following Sunday afternoon until the World Trade Center attack.'

Doug sat immobile, stunned. How stupid of him to think she'd gone through life alone all these years! To believe he could walk back into her life with simple words of explanation. 'I didn't know,' he whispered. 'How awful for her.'

'First and foremost,' Lisa began and broke off. 'No, I don't have a right to say any more—'

'Lisa, say it,' he pleaded, his eyes clinging to hers.

'Karen needs time to recover. Greg was very special, very important to her. Above all, her best friend.' Lisa's eyes sent a message she couldn't put into words. 'We went through school together. Two off-beat kids devoid of self-confidence. Then we both went away to college. We lost touch until she came home last month.'

'What should I do?'

'Wait,' Lisa urged. 'Give Karen some space.'

Twenty

In bed for the night, Doug stared at the ceiling and reviewed his day. Not the way to assure a decent night's sleep, he rebuked himself – it had been a traumatic day. Damn, when was the last time he'd gotten a decent night's sleep? Not once since he'd discovered Karen was in town.

Aside from the indirect contact with Karen today – which had sent his pulse going wild – he'd been in touch with the small-time investigator he'd hired to tail Cal Henderson. The guy had car trouble while on an assignment forty miles out of town – he'd missed the school lunch-time mob and the three p.m. school break. '*Hey, Doug, don't worry. I'll be there at lunch time tomorrow. If the creep's selling, I'll nail him.*'

And the talk with Sunshine's fancy New York lawyer had been disturbing. But he should have been prepared for that – after what Tony told him about a 'major contribution' to Hank Fredericks' campaign. The message he'd got from his conversation with the lawyer was that now the Sunshine people were nervous about the outcome of the election. They were demanding a meeting with the property owners, fighting for a quick settlement. But on their terms.

Sophie said one family was ready to accept, fighting with the other two to agree. '*They know I'll never go along with those bargain basement prices.*' And Sophie was right. To sell at the prices Sunshine was offering was to be the prize suckers of the year.

At last Doug drifted off to sleep. The alarm clock jolted him into wakefulness at 7 a.m. He lay immobile – without opening his eyes – for a few minutes. Reliving the encounter with Karen near the elementary school. She was as beautiful as she was all those years ago – that same vulnerable glow in her eyes.

Lisa's exhortation ricocheted in his brain: '*Wait. Give Karen some space.*'

All right – I won't try to approach her. But I'll hurry over to the florist market – they're already open. Take one red rose and lay it at Karen's door. Let her know that I'm here for her.

In her sprawling country kitchen Sophie poured coffee for the three couples who'd arrived – with an odd aura of menace – ten minutes ago. The plate of cookies she'd put on the table remained untouched.

'Sophie, we've been talking about this situation.' The brawny, middle-aged, long-distance truck driver who lived next door with his wife and three teenaged kids glanced about to include the others about the table. 'And we think we oughta go along with the Sunshine people. We'll get a lot more than we paid for our houses. And—'

'You've all been in your houses over twenty years,' Sophie broke in impatiently. 'The prices have gone way up through those years. Sunshine needs our property. It would be stupid to sell at what they're offering.'

'My son, the accountant,' another neighbor began, gazing about for an instant at the others for support, 'says we're being too independent. Tommy says they'll get disgusted and talk to property owners across the road. That one house has enough acreage to give Sunshine all the parking space they'll need.'

'It's across the street,' Sophie pinpointed. 'They don't want customers to have to cross the road. That would—'

'It'd be no problem,' a local plumber, who boasted about

144

finishing off his mortgage in another two years, pounced with an air of triumph. 'They'll build a viaduct over the road.'

'They don't want that kind of a deal.' Sophie's face was flushed. She wished Doug was here to talk to them. But there could be no sale without her going along with it. They needed her property for the entrance to a prospective parking lot. 'We'll get market price if we hold out.' And her expression told them she meant to do just that.

'Where's Joe these days?' the truck driver asked slyly. 'I hear he's left town.' The glint in his eyes said he suspected Joe of being involved with terrorists.

'He went down to New York to check on colleges there,' Sophie fabricated. 'To find out if he could enter as a local resident. You know – real cheap tuition.' She managed a smile. *They've known us for years – how dare they act as though we're Arab terrorists!* 'He's due home later this morning.'

Doug was impatient to be through with the closing which was being held in his office this morning. At intervals he sneaked a glance at his watch. Thank God, it was a routine closing. He'd wrap it up in another ten minutes. The seller's lawyer, too, seemed in a rush to be on his way. Probably headed for that Rotary lunch in town today. A strong supporter of Hank Fredericks, he remembered with distaste.

'That's it?' the wide-eyed young bride asked delightedly when Doug handed her the deed with congratulatory words.

'That's it.' A nice young couple, he thought in a corner of his mind while they exchanged a chaste kiss. The economy might be shaky, but the dropping mortgage rates – the lowest in many a year – had made it possible for them to buy. And for an euphoric instant he visualized Karen and himself buying a house – unless she'd be satisfied to renovate his parents' house – now his.

'Thanks for seeing us through this, Doug.' The recent

bridegroom extended a hand. 'You have to come over for dinner one night when we get settled in.'

'I'll look forward to that.' Doug walked with them to the door. The other lawyer was rushing his people out of the office now. The bank representative had dashed out first.

Doug was anxious for the chit-chat to be over, to learn if Cal had been doing business at the junior high school during lunch time. The investigator ought to be reporting by now.

The phone rang. Olivia picked up.

'The law offices of Doug Madison,' she chirped. 'Good morning.' She listened a moment. 'Oh, sure.' She turned to Doug. 'It's for you. The investigator you hired—'

'I'll take it in my office,' Doug told her and hurried to his desk phone. 'Hi, how'd you make out?'

'Caught him red-handed,' the investigator said with relish. 'I got the transaction on film – and I scared the kid into selling me his stash. I don't think you'll need more.'

'You'll be the witness,' Doug reminded. 'Pick me up here at the office. We've got a date with the Police Chief.'

Cal would serve time for dealing drugs. And that would destroy his credibility in Marty's case. Cal and his brother would not walk away from the beating they gave Marty Mohammed. No way could the Fredericks crowd white-wash those two creeps.

It was close to 6 p.m. before Doug was clear to head for campaign headquarters. This was the in-between period, he thought as he strode inside. The day people – except for the handful who worked from morning until they closed shop at anywhere from 10 p.m. to midnight – were taking off. The evening volunteers wouldn't show up for another hour.

'I saw you coming,' Tony greeted him. 'I ordered roast beef sandwiches and coffee.'

'Great.' Doug dropped exhausted into a chair.

'My wife – who says she feels like a widow these days – sent over a salad bowl and cookies.' Tony reached into a drawer to retrieve these.

'Don't complain,' Doug scolded. 'Edie's thrown three teas for us – and she's brought in donors.'

'I suspect we're going to see some heated action on Monday,' Tony reminded.

'You mean that emergency meeting at the elementary school.' Lisa had told them about how Karen had twisted Kendricks' arm. Doug had heard he wasn't happy about it – but he had called the meeting. To cover his ass, Doug interpreted. Kendricks didn't want an ugly hassle with *The Sentinel* – and instinct told him Karen would make it a big issue.

'There'll be parents – and teachers,' Tony warned, 'who're hostile. Who're convinced that the kids in the school must be made aware of actions by Arabs at the World Trade Center. They want those kids to be on guard against possible Arab terrorists.'

'Elementary-grade kids?' Doug scoffed. 'Here in Weston?'

'Remember, they're all watching television. They know their parents are unnerved. And we have an Arab-American community. Just a few families – but they stand out.'

'Kids have to be taught the difference between radical Arabs and Americans who happen to be of Arab descent!' Visualizing the frightened little girl taunted by those five little boys, Doug churned with fresh rage. 'And that has to start in the homes and carry over into the schools.'

'So let's work on that.' But Tony seemed dubious about the results.

'I want to speak at that emergency meeting,' Doug said in sudden decision.

'You think they'll let you?' Tony was skeptical.

'I'll put up a fight.' *Karen sold Kendricks on the meeting. Can I sell him – and the Parent Teacher Association – on allowing me to speak? It's a public forum. How can they deny it?*

Yet he knew there would be an uproar at this proposal.

Twenty-One

Karen lingered in bed on Saturday morning. She didn't have to go into the office today, though Mike had made it clear there would be long stretches where she would have no days off.

'*Between Monday and Election Day we'll be in there plugging non-stop. This election is too damn close for us to take time off.*'

She ought to be glad to have some free time, she chided herself – but the empty weekend ahead seemed an obstacle course. She needed to be busy – to have no time to think beyond the current task.

She'd talked with Sophie last evening. Sophie was so relieved that Joe was home, that Marty appeared convinced that he must remain in town. Marty and Joe were part of the civilian patrol that was providing protection for Arab-American families. And now, Sophie confided, she was at the Tony Mendoza campaign headquarters every moment she could manage.

Guilt tugged at Karen. This was such a critical campaign – and she still shied from volunteering. But she'd been of a little help, she thought, trying to bolster her shaky ego. She'd worked on editing Doug's mailing piece.

With a need for action she left the bed and began to prepare for the day. The apartment needed a real cleaning. She had laundry to do. Drive to the supermarket and load up. Mike had said they'd be working insane hours from now to Election Day. She'd have no time for grocery shopping.

From habit she paused to watch a segment of the national news. The whole world was upside-down – but why did newscasters keep repeating that the world we'd known was forever gone? That was frightening. After every disaster the world recovered and went on. But the country had changed in good ways, too. People everywhere were eager to be of help, to give of themselves. At least, many of them.

She cleaned with a vigor that was meant to ease her tension. With the apartment spotless, she settled down for a cup of tea. For a moment she considered watching a few more minutes of television news. No, the TV stations kept repeating the same news over and over. She wasn't a news junkie.

The phone rang – a jarring intrusion. She crossed to pick up the receiver.

'Hello.'

'Karen, we need some help,' Lisa said without preliminaries. 'Doug was up most of the night, I gather – and he's come up with some material he hopes to present at the emergency meeting Monday night. But he says it lacks—'

'Will they let him speak?' Karen was startled. She was to cover that meeting, along with a *Sentinel* photographer.

'Tony and a couple of the guys are working on it today. At any rate Doug feels he has to be prepared.' Lisa paused. 'Karen, will you work on the material again?'

'OK.' She struggled for poise. 'You'll bring it over to me?'

'Sure.' Relief in Lisa's voice.

'I have to run over to the supermarket,' Karen said. 'But I should be back in about an hour.'

'I'll bring over the material and lunch,' Lisa promised. 'In about an hour.'

Karen drove over to the local, independently-owned supermarket – conscious of the Sunshine chain's continuing fight to buy property for their parking area. Lisa said she was sure Mayor Fredericks wanted to see the deal go through because there'd be a hefty bonus for him.

She shopped hurriedly, chafing at the Saturday morning horde of shoppers. At intervals she overheard argumentative discussions about the coming election. Even up here, she thought, people seem stressed out by the September 11th attack. It hadn't affected just New Yorkers – the whole country felt the after affects.

Restless at the long lines, she waited her turn at the checkout counter. This morning she was conscious of the diversity of the town. Carts were being pushed by people of various nationalities. Accents here and there hinted at foreign birth. But wasn't that the natural make-up of an American town?

Relieved to be done with her shopping, she loaded the car trunk, drove back to her apartment. Laden down with parcels she saw Lisa approaching. Lisa was such a dynamo. So good for this town.

'Let me take a couple of those.' Lisa reached out for two plastic bags, meanwhile clutching the paper bag with their prospective lunch. 'I hope you're in the mood for veggie burgers. We've got this new health food shop in town. The burgers are huge and tasty.'

'If I don't have to make it, I'm in the mood for it,' Karen assured her. She was glad Lisa had called this morning. The day ahead seemed less dreary.

They sprawled on the sofa, with veggie burgers and mugs of coffee on the table. While they ate, Karen perused the material. She was caught up in what Doug was trying to say with a passion that would reach out to the doubtful.

'This is all true.' This was a special kind of torment, Karen told herself. To feel so close to Doug – and yet so far away.

'There's no guarantee he'll be allowed to speak,' Lisa conceded, 'but he could sway a lot of people into the right direction.'

'I'll re-type this,' Karen decided. 'When I finish with the revisions.'

'Tony said that Mike Canfield is writing a sizzling editorial on the election for tomorrow's *Sentinel*. If people start thinking logically about this situation, then maybe they'll go to the polls and vote logically.'

The inner circle of Tony Mendoza's campaign sat in his office on this unseasonably warm Sunday morning and waited for him to return from his meeting with Dr Kendricks in his school office.

'You did a great job of getting those signatures,' Mike congratulated Doug. 'Kendricks will have a hard time denying you permission to address the emergency meeting.'

'This is important,' Gloria, Tony's publicist, conceded. 'But at this point I'm more concerned about the election. Hank Fredericks' new radio commercials start blasting tomorrow morning. And the TV commercials. My "mole" tells me they're vicious.'

'That bastard Fredericks isn't out to win this election,' Tony's official Chief of Staff scoffed – though, in truth, Doug held this position. 'He means to buy it.'

Tony Mendoza's private phone rang. Doug grabbed it. 'Yeah?' His voice harsh with anxiety.

'You're speaking at the meeting,' Tony reported. 'The signatures and Mike's editorial spooked Kendricks. He didn't dare say no.'

Karen and her photographer, Steve, arrived at the elementary school twenty minutes before the emergency meeting was to begin. For a few moments she was engulfed in nostalgia. In all these years nothing seemed to have changed.

She remembered the years she'd spent in this school – always imprisoned by insecurity, her mother's exhortations to do this or that or 'the other kids will laugh at you.' And when teachers made complimentary remarks to her class about her, she'd wanted to crawl under the floor because that was making her different from the others.

Steve parked. He and Karen left the car. From the number of cars that sat in the parking area she suspected there would be a large turnout. And a steady stream of people were heading for the school entrance.

'I hope they've got the air-conditioning running.' Steve handed Karen his camera so he could remove his jacket. 'The summer doesn't want to end.'

'Maybe all those people warning about global warming deserve to be heard.' *Why am I so tense? Steve and I will be at the rear of the auditorium. Lisa said Doug will come in by the side entrance – just before Kendricks announces that he's to speak. I won't come face to face with Doug.*

But she couldn't erase from her mind the single red rose that lay at her door each morning. No mistake. Doug pleading his case.

Karen and Steve joined the throng going into the school, made their way into the auditorium, stationed themselves at the rear. Far to their right, Karen spied a team from *The Star*. Another photographer was adjusting his camera while he talked to a woman beside him. Coverage from a nearby town, Karen surmised. The word about the emergency meeting had traveled fast.

'The air-conditioning works,' Steve said in approval. 'So, it's almost mid-October – we need it.'

Part of Karen's mind was attuned to the conversations around them. These were people with strong opinions. The talk focused around the September 11th attack: *'Look, this is war. We can't pussyfoot around the enemy. I want my kids to know what's going on around them – and be watchful'*; *'We don't need a witchhunt here in town! Fredericks and his crew are creating an awful situation here with all their radio and TV commercials. Don't people learn from the past?'*

Then the president of the Parent Teacher Association

walked out on to the small stage. The audience abandoned chatter. The atmosphere electric.

'This meeting has been called because we must face a serious situation that has arisen in this town . . .'

Karen's eyes roamed about the audience as the woman on the stage reviewed the recent happenings in Weston. The tension level high. Then she introduced Dr Kendricks, and furtive whispering was heard here and there in the auditorium as he began to speak. Not everybody admired Kendricks, Karen remembered.

'What a windbag,' Steve muttered, but dutifully he was snapping photos for tomorrow's edition of *The Sentinel*.

Karen clenched her teeth in irritation as Dr Kendricks rambled on. As expected, he was taking no sides, issuing mild reproofs. She forced herself to make notes while she churned with frustration because he was avoiding the real issues at stake.

Glances about the auditorium told her that the audience was split. Some – along with Steve and herself – were disgusted with his apologies for the ugliness that had invaded the town. His plea for compassion. Others – in their minds – advocated something close to a police state.

'We must at all times be vigilant. Remember, we're at war. We never know who around us is plotting against our great country. We will not become victims!'

Huge applause broke out in some sectors. Others were silent, radiating rejection. Like the polls – warning that either side might win in the imminent election, Karen thought uneasily.

And then – in a stiff, self-conscious manner – Kendricks announced their guest speaker. Doug strode into the auditorium from the side entrance, made his way to the stage. Warm applause from one segment of the auditorium.

Doug took his place at the podium.

'I'm here,' he said, 'because our town is under attack. Not by foreign elements but from our very own. This must stop—'

Twenty-Two

Tears stinging her eyes, Karen listened to Doug's impassioned plea for the town to recognize what horrors were being committed in its midst. At intervals, bursts of applause. But those who weren't applauding – what were they thinking? Was Doug changing minds? Instinctively she knew that this meeting could have a huge effect on the voting. People would leave here and they would talk. Mayor Fredericks was basing his campaign on fears of foreign attacks: 'Be watchful – beware of enemies among us.' Fredericks was creating violence. Why can't everybody realize that?

She was startled when Doug announced a question-and-answer period. Dr Kendricks was taken aback, furious, she noted. But hands were shooting up. Questions flew at Doug – some friendly, some hostile. Fighting to conceal his rage, Kendricks at last came forward to call the meeting closed.

'I'm rushing back to the paper,' Steve said, then hesitated. They'd arrived in his car. 'But you'll need a ride home . . .'

'Go,' Karen said. 'I have just a twenty-minute walk home. I need the exercise.'

She lingered for a moment to exchange conversation with the woman who'd recently opened the health food store.

'Every word Doug Madison said was true,' the storekeeper said with conviction. 'And let's hope when people go to the polls in three weeks, they'll remember.'

Karen saw Doug surrounded by people as he walked down from the stage. And she knew his eyes had found her. Her heart pounding, she turned to leave. Her passage slow because of the cluster of people pausing in conversation. She breathed a sigh of relief when she emerged into the night air.

'Karen!' The urgency in Doug's voice brought her to a halt. She stood immobile while he charged to her side. 'Karen, I know you've been revising my material. You're so good at that. You always were . . .' For a moment their eyes clung, then Karen turned away.

'There wasn't much required.' *Why am I standing here talking with him this way?*

'The campaign needs you,' he said quietly. 'The polls scare the hell out of me. And we're running out of funds – at a time when Fredericks just got a huge infusion.'

'I–I'm busy with my job on *The Sentinel*,' she stammered. *He knows I'm working on the paper, doesn't he?*

'Just a couple of hours in the evening,' he pleaded. 'In these last three weeks.' He took a deep breath. 'This town can't afford another term under Hank Fredericks.'

'I–I don't know—'

'Karen, you can make a difference. The corruption we've seen in the past eight years is unbelievable. Let's talk about it over coffee,' he implored. 'If we lose this campaign, a lot of people will be hurting.'

'All right—' *I'm out of my mind.*

'My car's over there.' He pointed across the parking area. 'I can drive you back here after coffee to pick up your car.'

'I drove over with Steve, the paper's photographer,' she explained, walking with him to his car. *Why did I agree to have coffee with him?*

Sitting beside Doug in the car, she berated herself for being here with him. It was though they'd hurtled back through the years, and she was holding the phone and hearing him say those awful words: '*Karen, I'm so sorry.*

156

Something's happened. I have to leave school. I'm getting married.'

While they drove, Doug talked about the campaign, the underhanded tricks the Fredericks crew threw at them. 'There are a lot of people praying we'll clean up local government. And now this "hate Arabs" scene threatens to cause some division. There's a kind of hysteria in the air that we've never seen in this country.'

At this hour of the evening Doug found a parking spot before the one café in town that was open 24 hours. They left the car and walked into the well-populated café. Karen recognized faces from the school auditorium. Hands rose to wave to Doug in warm greeting.

They were guided to a small booth at the rear. Doug was known here, Karen realized as he exchanged banter with their waitress.

'Strong black coffee,' the waitress trilled before he could order, 'and cherry cheesecake.' Then she turned to Karen.

'The same for me.' Karen managed a tentative smile. *He still drinks black coffee and likes cherry cheesecake.*

When they were alone again, Doug told her about the progress of the civilian patrol. And then his face relaxed into a gentle grin. 'Guess where Sophie and Amy Lansing are this evening? The two of them are out on a special campaign,' he told her before she could reply. 'They're over in the African-American sections of town with our new fliers and persuasive talk. Amy says minority voters have to stick together – and that means votes for Tony and his slate.'

'Sophie's very bright – and very brave.'

'Sometimes I wish she was a little less brave,' Doug said wryly.

'I can probably be at campaign headquarters most evenings.' Karen fought for an impersonal tone. 'Unless something comes up at the paper that I have to cover.'

'That's terrific!' For a moment he glowed. Then – as

though he was fearful of showing too much emotion – he retreated. 'Tony will be so grateful.'

Now – as though by mutual agreement – they concentrated on campaign talk. With cake and coffee out of the way, Doug drove her home. He was being so careful not to push himself, Karen thought – and was touched by this. Still, she was fearful of going beyond this business-like relationship.

I won't allow myself to be hurt again. I've struck out twice. That's enough.

In the room of the old Victorian house that Hank Fredericks liked to call the library – by virtue of the set of the Encyclopedia Britannica and several politically-oriented hardcovers whose pages were still uncut – he sat hunched behind his oversized desk and scowled at the two men sprawled on the red velvet Victorian sofa.

'Damnit, this election is becoming a pain in the ass! Three weeks from today voters will be going to the polls. By this time on Election Day they'll have a pretty good idea about who'll be running the town for the next two years. Six months ago we were sure we had it sewed up. And now that bastard Mendoza is breathing down our necks.'

'Boss, you're gonna win,' the older of the two men – who did odd jobs for Fredericks – predicted. But his air of bravado was shaky. They know, Hank thought, if I don't win this election, they're out in the cold.

'And how come Sunshine can't tie up the deal with the houses?' Fredericks demanded – but it was a rhetorical question. He sent them a sly smile. 'I told you – once it goes through, you get a nice bonus. You did okay with three of the houses – scaring them into thinking they might lose out to the property across the road. But we've still one major problem—'

'Sophie Mohammed – she's the stumblin' block,' the older man admitted. 'That no-good Arab.'

'Do something about her,' Fredericks ordered. 'You hear how she and old lady Lansing have been going after our "minority" citizens? Canvassing door to door,' he said contemptuously. 'Telling them they have to get to the polls to vote.' His face tightened. 'And not for me.'

'It would kinda be a shame,' the older man drawled, 'if Sophie Mohammed's house burnt to the ground. Wouldn't it?'

Fredericks grunted impatiently. 'No more fires. What I worry about,' he said meaningfully, 'is the way she's going after folks who never bother to go out and vote. Now why should they put themselves out to vote now?'

'You mean on Election Day we hafta make sure they don't vote?' The younger man grinned. 'Hey, we can handle that.'

'Do something about Sophie Mohammed.' Fredericks' eyes narrowed in thought. 'Go home and think about it.' He paused. 'Talk to Jake.' (His silent lieutenant that others in the party preferred not to notice.) 'He's real sharp.'

Sophie gazed at her two sons with pleasure as they devoured the fish wrapped in grape leaves she'd prepared for dinner. She scolded them at regular intervals for the fast food they settled for at lunch time.

'Mom, you're eating that rabbit food again,' Joe scolded.

'At least she doesn't have to drive thirty-eight miles to get it now,' Marty ribbed affectionately. 'I think she's trying to keep the new health food shop in town in business.'

'Veggie burgers are not rabbit food.' Sophie glanced at the clock. 'And the two of you have to get off to your civilian patrol duty in a few minutes.' She was proud they'd both volunteered – though it had taken some prodding on Joe's part. But, thank God, he'd come home. He was over that craziness about going to fight with bin Laden. 'How do you both happen to be on duty tonight?'

'Somebody's down with a virus – Mike Canfield sent me

an SOS to fill in,' Marty explained. 'So I won't watch TV tonight.' He shrugged this off. 'An extra four-hour shift this week won't kill me.'

'Mom, you shouldn't be running around in bad neighborhoods at night.' Joe was somber. 'I don't like it.'

'Who has to like? And don't call it a "bad neighborhood." Just a neighborhood where people don't have much money. I don't go alone,' she reminded. 'I go with Amy Lansing. And don't ask why we don't go in the daytime. I have a shop to run. Besides, as Amy pointed out, in the evening we get to talk to the whole family.'

'Our mother the politician,' Marty joshed. Still, she knew he was proud of her activities.

Joe was fidgeting in his chair. 'Mom, what's going to happen with the house?'

'We wait until the Sunshine lawyer tells Doug they're meeting our price.' An air of defiance in her voice now.

'The others are willing to go along,' Joe reminded her.

'We're not,' Marty flashed back. 'Why have you got ants in your pants about the sale?'

'It's just that the others are pissed at us.' Joe frowned. 'I was supposed to take Jeannie Ford to the movies last night – and she dumped me. She said her folks couldn't figure out why we're holding up the sale.' He hesitated. 'It's not that some folks in town hate us because we're Arab-Americans.'

'We're Americans,' Sophie corrected, 'who happen to be of Arab descent. We're proud of that,' she emphasized, 'but we look on fanatic Arabs as scum.'

Marty pushed back his chair. 'Okay, let's get cracking. You're not going electioneering tonight, Mom.' It was more an order than a question.

'No,' Sophie promised. 'I'll go over to headquarters for a couple of hours, stuff some more envelopes.'

With Marty and Joe off for civilian patrol duty, Sophie cleared the table, stacked the dishwasher. There was a faint chill in the air. She would take a sweater in case the temperature dropped another few degrees. Would the boys be warm enough? They never seemed to feel the cold.

Joe was upset about Jeannie's breaking a date with him, she thought compassionately as she walked to her bedroom. He and Jeannie had been going together almost a year now. Nothing real serious, she told herself. Joe knew it was important for him to get a college degree.

With her sweater tied about her waist Sophie headed for her car in the driveway. She'd been right to take the sweater. The wind was high. Not a star in the sky tonight. Not even a sliver of a moon.

All at once the night quiet that she loved was splintered by the crunch of a broken bough. A few weeks ago she would have dismissed this as the approach of a squirrel or some other small animal.

'Who's there?' Her voice sharp, wary.

Then something was thrown over her head. Strong arms lifted her from her feet. She struggled, but the effort was futile.

'Let me go! Let me go!' In a corner of her mind, a voice ordered her not to panic. 'Who are you? Where are you taking me?'

Twenty-Three

Marty grimaced as his alarm clock shrieked its 6 a.m. message. He'd finished his stint on the civilian patrol last night at midnight, hadn't got to bed until close to one a.m. He yawned, pulled the comforter over his shoulders. OK, take another five minutes.

He heard rain pounding on the roof, remembered the drizzle that had fallen in the last hour of his patrol. The civilian patrol traveled in pairs, staked out before the houses of the families they were guarding. Since word got around about the patrol, he thought with satisfaction, there'd been no further incidents. But how long would they have to keep this up?

With reluctance he tossed aside the comforter. No use stalling. Maybe he'd turn up the thermostat, bring up some heat for awhile. Mom liked the house to be warm. He listened for sounds in the kitchen. Mom was up with Joe and him every morning – even though she didn't open the shop until ten. She took care of the house, made breakfast for them, put in half a day's work before her business day even started, he thought lovingly.

He headed for the thermostat in the hall, pushed it up, heard the comforting rumble that said the house would soon be warm. Nice thing about this house, he thought complacently as he strode into the bathroom. It warmed up fast.

'Hey, Joe,' he called from the bathroom door. 'Get the lead out – this is a working day.'

He ran a hot shower, stepped beneath the stinging spray. In another three months this job would be completed, he warned himself with simmering apprehension. Everybody talked about the shitty economy. When would he and Joe latch on to jobs again?

In roughly eleven months he meant to be in architectural school. He needed every cent he could put his hands on. Mom was sharp – she'd refinanced the house when mortgage rates fell. She said she could increase the mortgage to help him and Joe with college. He'd been hoping for a great deal with Sunshine.

'Marty!' Joe banged on the bathroom door. 'Get the hell out here!'

'What's with you?' Marty yelled back, switched off the water and grabbed for a towel. He opened the door. 'What's up?'

'Mom's not home.' Joe's face was drained of color.

'What do you mean – she's not home?'

'She's not in her room. Her bed hasn't been slept in. Marty, some bastards took her!' Joe's voice was shrill.

'That's nuts!' Marty strode past him to their mother's bedroom off to one side of the house. When they got home last night, he'd glanced down the hall from habit – to see if she was awake. The room had been dark.

'We go out and patrol for everybody else – and we leave Mom alone! Where the hell is she?'

'We'll call the cops,' Marty said, then paused. 'We'll call Doug.'

The two raced to the phone in the kitchen. Marty punched in Doug's home number. It was early to awaken him – but Doug would understand, Marty told himself. He clutched the receiver tightly while the phone rang at the other end.

'What's happening?' Joe demanded.

'It's ringing – give him a chance.' But Marty understood the terror his brother was feeling. Terror that invaded him as well.

'Hello.' Doug was struggling to come awake.

'Doug, it's me. Marty. Mom's gone. Joe and I came home from patrol late last night. Mom's room was dark – we thought she was asleep.' He paused, stared out a kitchen window. 'Her car's here – sitting in the driveway!'

'Ask him if we should call the police,' Joe said.

'Should we call the police?' Marty asked.

'They won't consider it a "missing person" situation for forty-eight hours,' Doug dismissed.

'Even with what's been happening in town?' Marty challenged in soaring anger. 'Damn, we shouldn't have left Mom alone. She's one of the people we've been appointed to guard!'

'Cool it, Marty,' Doug soothed. 'We'll find her.'

'Last night she said she was going over to campaign headquarters,' Marty recalled. 'Did you see her last night?'

'No. I presumed she was out electioneering with Amy Lansing again. Stay there, Marty. I'm coming over.'

With a need for action, Marty put up a pot of coffee while Joe paced and swore. In ten minutes they heard a car pull up before the house. They hurried to the door. Doug was emerging from his car. He stared at the ground as he strode towards the house.

'If there were any footprints, the rain has washed them away,' Doug pointed out as he walked into the house. 'All right, let's sit down and try to figure out which way we should go.'

With morning sunlight pouring into the one-room cabin after a rain-drenched night, Sophie emerged from chaotic dozing. Instantly she was aware of the circumstances that had brought her here. She sat motionless in the decrepit club chair that had been her bed for the night. Her feet – loosely tied with rope – rested on a makeshift hassock. Her hands in handcuffs.

'You want some tea?' a light, feminine voice asked with

an excited yet giggly tone. 'I ain't good at makin' coffee.'

'Why am I here?' Sophie demanded of the lanky yet pretty teenager who hovered before her. 'You're going to be in big trouble!'

'I don't know nothin'.' Sophie's sole guard giggled. 'I'm jest to keep you in that chair. Except when you need to go to the bathroom over there.' She pointed to a corner of the room, then reached for a shotgun that Sophie had not noticed until this moment. 'I'm a good shot – better than some guys. I did a lotta practicin' at the quarry. And you needn't yell,' she continued, 'because there ain't nobody around for acres and acres.' She took a deep breath. 'Now you want some tea?'

'Yes.' Sophie forced herself to smile 'What's your name?'

'Lulie.' All at once her blue eyes were troubled. 'I ain't sure I shoulda told you that.'

'It'll be our secret,' Sophie promised. *She can't be more than 15 – and retarded. I should be able to outwit her, escape from this insanity.* 'I won't tell the others.'

'I'll git your tea.' Lulie seemed mollified as she crossed to the kerosene stove that stood in a corner of the cabin. 'And I make real good scrambled eggs.'

'That'll be good.' *I must play along with her. Wait for a moment when my hands are free – try to break out of here.*

Sophie's mind jolted into high gear. Two men were involved in kidnapping her. She'd heard them talking to each other when they brought her here. They'd left her tied up this way – and from exhaustion, she surmised, she finally fell asleep.

What do they want of me? If they meant to kill me, they could have done that last night.

Doug and Marty sat at the dining table in the kitchen while Joe paced.

'The police ought to be doing something!' Joe raged. 'We're living in crazy times. They know what's been

165

happening around here to Americans who – who have Arab backgrounds.'

'I'll call the DA's office,' Doug capitulated. He was sure they'd take no action at this point, but let Marty and Joe know that no possibility would be overlooked. 'No, I'll call the DA at home.' The office wouldn't open for another hour.

'We shouldn't have left her alone,' Marty railed. 'You told us not to leave her alone. We should have been here for her.'

The DA would be annoyed at this early call, Doug warned himself. And he wasn't exactly in favor at this point. He clutched the phone while it rang without response for what seemed minutes.

'Yeah, what's up?' The DA was surly at this disturbance.

'Sorry to wake you up,' Doug apologized, 'but we have a kidnapping here in town.'

'Who and when?' the DA snapped.

'Sophie Mohammed.' That wouldn't put a smile on his face, Doug thought. 'Her sons just reported she's been kidnapped.'

'They got a ransom note?' the DA asked edgily.

'No,' Doug admitted. This was going along the lines he'd expected. 'But she's missing. Her bed wasn't slept in. Her car's sitting in the driveway.'

'Doug, you know the routine,' the DA dismissed this. 'Unless there're definite signs of kidnapping we can't consider it a "missing persons" report for forty-eight hours. If she doesn't surface by tomorrow evening, we'll put men on the case.' Doug heard the phone slam down at the other end.

'The DA won't order an investigation before tomorrow evening,' Doug told Marty and Joe.

'Then we'll investigate!' Marty slammed a fist on the table. 'We've got to find her before—' He took a deep breath. 'Before they hurt her.'

'I'm calling Mike Canfield at *The Sentinel*.' Doug's mind

was racing ahead. 'We have to get the word around that your mother's missing. We'll—'

'*The Sentinel* won't come out until tomorrow morning.' Marty turned to Joe. 'Let's get fliers out all over town. Go dig up a snapshot of Mom.'

'Shouldn't somebody stay by the phone? In case they – they call with some demand?' Joe was fighting for composure. 'We could raise cash quick on the house.'

'This isn't some ransom deal,' Marty said impatiently. 'You know that, Joe!'

'What do they want?' Joe's eyes swung from his brother to Doug.

'We have to figure out who wants your mother out of the way,' Doug began, and Marty grunted.

'Maybe half this town,' Joe seethed.

'Let's zero in more tightly,' Doug ordered. 'Beyond the sick fanatics who've grabbed on the Arab question, who should we consider? There's the Fredericks crew – because your mother has been out there with Amy Lansing to bring in the minority vote – which in a tight election like this could be the determining factor. Then there's the Sunshine people – furious that she's holding up the sale. And your three neighbors,' he added grimly, 'who're scared they'll lose a sale. At this point let's consider all of them as possible perpetrators.'

'Mom's been so good to this town!' Joe shook head in frustration.

'Let's start working.' Doug reached for the phone. 'I'm calling *The Sentinel* to make sure they run a front-page story in tomorrow morning's edition. You two rustle up a snapshot, list some vital statistics. Height, hair, age – what she might be wearing. One of you run over to the copy center on Main, have them run off a thousand copies and wait for them. We need to plaster them all over town.' He'd call Amy Lansing, urge her to set up a team to help circulate the fliers.

167

'Go find a photo of Mom,' Marty told Joe. 'I'll work out the flier copy.'

'Where am I going to find a snapshot?' Joe was white with fear.

'The album Mom keeps in her bedroom,' Marty told him. 'Get moving. I'll set up the copy.' He reached into a drawer where Sophie kept paper and pens.

Doug glanced at his watch. Mike was known to be at his office at ungodly early hours. If he wasn't there, call him at home. He reached for the phone, punched in Mike's private number at his office.

'Where's the fire?' Mike's voice – good-humored despite the hour – came to him after the second ring.

'Trouble, Mike,' Doug said. 'Sophie Mohammed's missing.'

'Oh, shit! Since when?'

'Marty and Joe got home late last night – from civilian patrol. They thought she was asleep. This morning she wasn't in the house. Her bed hadn't been slept in – her car's out in the driveway. We're getting out fliers to slap around town.'

'The police won't play yet,' Mike guessed. 'I'll need a photo for a front-page story. Doug, this is nuts!'

'I'll have Joe drop off a photo for you,' Doug began, and then paused in thought. 'No, send somebody over to work up a story for tomorrow's paper. Damn it, this town has got to turn out to find her.'

'I'll send somebody over as soon as I can get a call through,' Mike promised. 'Notify the radio station and the TV station. This is major news.'

'Right,' Doug agreed. 'And we can use some help with distributing the fliers, Mike.'

'Have Joe leave a bunch with me – I'll put some guys on it. Stay by the phone, Doug. Not that I expect any ransom calls,' Mike conceded. 'I'd feel happier if I thought there would be calls.'

Off the phone with Mike, Doug called Amy – known to be an early riser.

'Amy, I've got lousy news,' Doug apologized. 'Sophie Mohammed is missing. We—'

'Doug, we have to find her!' Amy broke in. 'I was afraid of something like this. What about circulating fliers?'

'In work. Will you dig up a team to take them around? I can send over five hundred within an hour,' Doug estimated.

'Make it a thousand. We need to work fast. Meanwhile, I'll get on the phone.'

Marty had assembled copy for their flier, offered it for Doug's approval. 'Doug, what about the shop?' he asked, suddenly suspicious. 'You think they've done anything there?'

'Take a fast run over and look around. I'll stay here.' In the unlikelihood that a call came in. And Mike was sending over a reporter.

'Yeah. Joe!' Marty yelled. 'Let's go. I'll drive you over to the copy center and then check on the store.'

Joe charged into the kitchen. 'You think they did something to the shop?'

'We won't know till I check it out. Move it!'

While Marty and Joe charged out of the house, Doug reached for the phone again. Call the radio station and the television station. It was important to get the word out fast. He waited impatiently till he was put through to the news department at the radio station, reported that Sophie was missing.

'Doug, we can't run it until it's a police matter,' the news editor demurred. 'Ten to one she's sleeping over at a friend's house. Her kids forgot and got panicky.'

'In today's climate we—'

'Sorry, we can't run it yet. But thanks for calling it in.'

Frustrated, Doug called the television station's news department – with the same results.

Damn, both the radio and the TV people are in Hank Fredericks' pockets. All that air time the Fredericks campaign is buying.

Twenty-Four

Mike drummed the fingers of one hand on his desk while he waited for someone to respond to the phone.

'Hello.'

'Donna?' Mike asked.

'Yeah, Mike.'

'Get Pat on the line. I've got a rush assignment for him.'

'I was waiting a little while to call you,' Donna said. 'Pat's down with a case of the flu. He's running a 103 temperature.'

'When did this happen?' Just what he needed this morning.

'Pat was feeling lousy yesterday, but he insisted on going in to work.' A mild reprimand in her voice. Everybody knew Mike didn't coddle his people.

'Tell him to take care of himself, Donna. Sorry he's sick.'

Mike put down the phone. They had what he liked to call a streamlined staff – which meant they were down to the wire in the number of people on the payroll. He shouldn't send Arnie into a case like this, he cautioned himself. Arnie had all the subtlety of a rhino. And his writing wasn't exactly inspired.

Karen, he pinpointed with relief. She'd do a better job than Pat. This was her cup of tea. She knew Sophie. She'd put passion into the article. But who the hell had nabbed Sophie? he asked himself with rising apprehension as he reached for the phone, called Karen.

'Hello.' A fresh-from-slumber sound in her voice.

'Karen, I've got a rush assignment for you. Pat's down with the flu. Anyway, I think you're right for this one. It's a shocker,' he warned. 'Sophie Mohammed is missing.'

'Oh, my God!'

'I want you to go over to the house – hang around there, see what's happening. We'll run the story on tomorrow's front page. And I want you to stay on it until Sophie's found. Got it?'

'Got it.' But Karen sounded shaken, he thought. He didn't feel great himself.

'Keep in touch. I want to know everything that happens,' Mike ordered. 'Every tiny development.'

'Mike.' Karen hesitated. 'Do you believe some Arab-hating fanatic is behind this?'

'Sophie makes waves. It could be that – or something altogether different. We won't know,' he said grimly, 'until we find Sophie.'

Marty dropped Joe off at the copy center, headed for the shop. This was a nightmare, he thought – sick with shock. Mom – who was always out to help people – snatched away in the middle of the night. No, sometime in the evening – her bed hadn't been slept in.

He pulled into a parking area a few doors down from the shop, hurried there with a sense of foreboding. Nothing appeared wrong from the outside, he noted, while he reached into a pocket for the shop key. Nadine wouldn't be in until ten, he remembered – he'd have to call her and tell her what had happened. And just yesterday Mom had called off the night watchman.

He walked into the shop, gazing about for any sign of vandalism. Nothing out of line so far. He walked back into the small office. Mom and Nadine had left the computer on, he noted, and crossed to close it down. But the letter on the over-sized monitor captured his attention. He read in shock, re-read it, then – his hands trembling in disbelief – printed out the letter:

Dear Marty and Joe,
   I cant deal with whats hapening in this town. Im scared of what will come next. Plese forgive me. I have to get away. Dont wory about me. I will be OK.
Mom.

Marty held the printout in his hands and re-read it yet again. *I don't believe Mom wrote this. Somebody wants us to think she's run away. I don't believe this!*
He called the house. Doug answered.
'I'm in the shop,' Marty said. 'Somebody left the office computer on.' He took a deep breath. 'There was a letter addressed to Joe and me. From Mom. It's a set-up, Doug,' he said with fresh outrage. 'The letter says Mom ran off – she couldn't cope. That isn't Mom. She's a fighter.'
'Come home,' Doug ordered. 'Bring the printout.'

Having dressed in record time, Karen hurried from her apartment to her car. Hearing Mike say that Sophie was missing had brought in sharp focus the horror of those days in early September – always just under the surface. When would this insanity be over?
She drove to the Mohammed house. Her mind in chaos. *Please God, let Sophie be all right. This isn't a kidnapping for ransom. This is more of the anti-Arab madness.*
Pulling up before the house, she saw Sophie's car in the driveway – and another car parked at one side. Doug's car, she recognized. Her heart began to pound.
Even this morning she'd found the single red rose at her door. No doubt in her mind that it had been left there by Doug. A silent but eloquent statement that he was there for her – if she could bring herself to accept him. But this was not the time for personal anguish. Sophie was missing.

The front door swung open. Doug stood there. He must have heard the car drive up.

'Any word?' Karen called breathlessly as she hurried to the house.

'Nothing so far.' Doug's face was taut. A question showing in his eyes.

'Mike called me,' Karen explained. 'We'll run a front-page story in tomorrow's edition. He wanted me to do the story.'

'There's not much to tell so far,' Doug told her and – while they walked into the house – reported the little that was known. 'In some way this is linked to what happened at the World Trade Center,' Doug surmised, 'but I get vibes that say there's more to it than that.'

'You believe somebody broke into the shop and left that letter on the computer?' Karen probed. They must keep away from personal feelings, she exhorted herself. They were just two people anxious to find Sophie.

'There's no way anybody can convince me Sophie ran out. That would be totally out of character.' Doug paused, stiffened in alertness at the sound of a car pulling into the driveway. 'That's probably Marty.'

Moments later Marty strode into the house. 'Here's the printout,' he told Doug tersely after a quick greeting to Karen. 'Mom didn't write this.'

Doug took the printout. He held it so that he and Karen scanned it simultaneously.

'Sophie didn't write that,' Karen agreed. 'Look at the spelling errors.' Sophie took pride in her perfect spelling, her English grammar. 'Can't you take this to the police as evidence that she'd been abducted?'

'Not until tomorrow evening. The cops will stick to that forty-eight-hour rule.' Doug turned to Marty. 'Call whoever will be opening the shop this morning. Warn her not to touch the computer. The cops may find fingerprints there.'

'Oh hell, I haven't called Nadine,' Marty remembered.

'Do it now. And make sure she steers clear of the computer,' Doug reiterated. 'It mustn't be touched.'

'Is there a computer here in the house?' Karen asked.

'Yeah, in my room,' Marty told her.

'I know we don't have much evidence yet – but Mike's allowing most of the front page for the article. I'd like to do some background on your mother, Marty. Can we work on that now? Together?'

'Sure. As soon as I've called Nadine.' Marty turned to Doug. 'What about the letter? Can't you show it to the cops? So it isn't forty-eight hours – we've got proof positive that somebody's out to make us think Mom took off on her own.'

'I'll go over to the DA's office.' But Doug's face exuded skepticism. 'Though I'm *persona non grata* over there. But first I'll call Tony Mendoza. He'll jump on the bandwagon with us.'

The phone rang. Marty leaned forward to hit the speakerphone button.

'Hello.'

'This is Mike Canfield over at *The Sentinel*. Is Doug Madison there?'

'Yeah, one sec . . .'

'What's up?' Doug asked.

'Somebody left an envelope for our Lost and Found,' Mike said. 'It had an ATM card in it. Sophie's.'

'Who left it?'

'Some kid, the receptionist said. That's a plant, Doug,' Mike said with conviction. 'Somebody wants us to believe Sophie withdrew money, skipped town.'

'That's something else to take to the DA,' Marty pounced. 'That phony letter – and now the ATM card – that was supposed to make us believe Mom withdrew cash to help her run away.'

'How could strangers use Sophie's bank card? They'd have to know her code.' Karen was suspicious about this new development – then all at once terrified. Had Sophie been forced to divulge this? She saw this fear reflected in the others.

'I'm going to the DA's office.' Doug tried for an air of calm. 'They can check with the bank to see if there was a withdrawal. Probably not. But call Nadine,' he reminded Marty. 'Tell her not to go near the computer.'

'Doug, you're spinning your wheels,' the DA reproached. 'This isn't even a "missing person" case yet.'

'We need to know if Sophie withdrew money,' Doug insisted. 'If she did, then I'm off your back.'

'You're a pain in the ass.' But the DA was on the phone already.

The two men waited for a return call from Sophie's bank. A few minutes later a bank employee called.

'Yeah, she withdrew money,' he confirmed. 'Five hundred dollars at eight minutes past nine last night.'

Twenty-Five

Sitting at Marty's computer, Karen glanced out a bedroom window at the sound of a car. Doug was back from the DA's office. She rushed out to the living room. Marty was coming back into the house from the backyard, where he'd been working on some project. Joe had been hovering over the phone, willing it to ring.

'What happened?' Marty was opening the door as Doug strode up to the house.

'I can't figure it out,' Doug admitted. 'The DA was pissed that I asked, but he got in touch with the bank.'

'So what about it?' Joe churned with impatience.

'There was a withdrawal—' Doug paused. 'She withdrew five hundred dollars around nine last night.'

'How?' Karen was astounded. 'I don't believe this!'

'If they hurt Mom, I'll find them and I'll kill them!' Joe vowed.

'Do either of you know her code?' Karen probed, her mind in high gear.

Marty's face brightened. 'She figured nothing bad could happen in this town. She just used her name – you know, it's six digits.' He blew out in relief. 'Those bastards guessed she'd used something simple. She didn't tell them,' he emphasized. 'They guessed.'

'That's part of the frame – to make it seem Mom's run off.' Joe spread his hands in frustration. 'What do we do now?'

'You go over to the copy center and have more fliers made up,' Marty told him. 'Take money from the jar in the kitchen. Then start taping the fliers up wherever you see an empty wall.'

'What are you going to do?' Joe demanded, but he was heading for the kitchen.

'I'm calling on our neighbors – including your girl-friend's parents. Maybe they know something they haven't got around to telling us—' Marty hesitated. 'Maybe I should stay here to man the phone.'

'Go ask questions,' Doug urged. 'I'll stay here.' He reached into his jacket pocket for his cell phone, punched in numbers. 'I'll use this to keep in touch with my office.'

'Mike told me to stay with the story until your mother is home again. And I still need your help building up some more background material,' Karen reminded Marty.

'As soon as I return,' he promised.

'OK.' All at once Karen was disconcerted at the prospect of being alone in the house with Doug. A kind of exqui-site torment.

'I won't be long.' Marty was apologetic. 'I need to know that the neighbors in the Sunshine deal aren't keeping anything back from us.'

'You suspect the Sunshine people?' Karen was aston-ished.

'I suspect everybody in this town,' Marty said bluntly, then managed a weak smile. 'Except you and Doug.'

By 1 p.m. the town had been covered with fliers. Marty returned to the house frustrated.

'Our great neighbors are as hostile as hell – they're scared they won't make the deal of the year. At the same time they're scared for Mom. But they don't know a thing.'

For almost an hour, Karen and Marty conferred about Sophie's background. Karen was plagued with misgivings. Was she the right person to be doing the article when it was so important? She mustn't say anything that could be misconstrued by the unsympathetic in this town. Now the four of them sat in the living room in varying degrees of frustration.

'Joe, run out for a pizza for our lunch,' Doug told him, extending a bill. 'We need clear heads,' he jibed gently because Joe seemed affronted at the prospect of eating.

'I'll put up coffee.' Karen rose to her feet – relieved by this activity.

'I'll be back in a bit.' Marty headed for the rear of the house.

Karen lingered in the kitchen. She was terrified for Sophie – and fighting panic at being alone with Doug. On those inadvertent moments when their eyes met, she felt his desperate hope of breaking down the wall between them.

Almost simultaneously, Joe returned with the pizza and Marty from the project that had taken him into the backyard. Karen came from the kitchen with plates and cutlery – just as Marty unrolled a large sign: MISSING: SOPHIE MOHAMMED. $10,000 REWARD FOR INFORMATION LEADING TO HER RETURN.

'What do you think?' Marty appealed to the others. 'I'm putting it on the pick-up truck and driving it around town.'

'Marty, where the hell are we going to get ten thousand dollars?' Joe gaped at him in alarm.

'We've got Mom's power of attorney,' Marty told him and Doug nodded.

'I drew up the form two days ago,' Doug said. 'Your mother wanted to be sure you two could deal with it if something happened to her.'

'She saw what was going on, and she wanted to be sure you'd have access to all of her assets should something – something unexpected occur.' Always Sophie was concerned for the welfare of her sons, she thought tenderly.

'You should have no trouble getting a fast loan on the

business or the house,' Doug pointed out. 'At least one bank in town is not supporting Hank Fredericks.'

'But don't apply until you need the money,' Karen cautioned, and Doug nodded in agreement.

'Make it fifty thousand,' Joe ordered Marty. 'Change the one to a five.'

'A piece of cake.' Marty rolled up the sign again, preparing to return to the backyard.

'Wait,' Karen ordered. 'Cold pizza isn't a gourmet delight.'

Sophie watched while Lulie hovered at the kerosene cookstove – striving not to burn the scrambled eggs and bacon that seemed to be her one culinary accomplishment.

Lulie is a sweet, misguided, retarded 15-year-old girl. Why can't I manage to get out of here when she takes off the handcuffs? So my ankles are tied together – I can hobble out of here if I can manage to tie her up.

Sophie's eyes darted about the room, then settled on Lulie. On the scarf Lulie wore about her waist. *Try to pin her down, grab the scarf. She won't be expecting me to do that.*

'I'm so hungry, Lulie,' Sophie said with wistful charm. 'But it's so hard to eat with the cuffs on.'

'I'll take 'em off – just long enough for you eat,' Lulie decided. 'But don't you try nothin',' she warned.

Tense, alert to what she was about to attempt, Sophie waited for Lulie to divide the eggs and bacon into two portions, slide them on to plates. Lulie brought one plate to the much-scratched end table that sat beside Sophie's chair, reached into her pocket for the handcuff key. *Pin her arms behind her – reach for the scarf. She's tiny and slight – I can do it.*

Every nerve tingling, Sophie held up handcuffed hands. Lulie paused, shifted the key to her left hand, leaned over to pick up the shotgun that sat against the wall. With the shotgun positioned in her right hand – pointing to Sophie's heart, Lulie maneuvered the key and handcuffs with her left hand.

'You be good, Sophie,' Lulie said, releasing the hand-cuffs, ''cause I don't wanna shoot you. And I'm a better shot than—' She stopped in sudden alarm. 'I ain't gonna say his name – but he's real good.'

'I won't do anything,' Sophie promised and reached for the plate of scrambled eggs and bacon. So much for that attempt. 'Do you suppose I could have a cup of tea – or coffee?'

'We got tea bags. You had tea before,' she reminded her. 'Finish your eggs, lemme put back the handcuffs, then I'll make your tea.'

Pleased with this decision Lulie took her position with the shotgun while Sophie ate.

Why are they keeping me here? How long will they hold me? What are they after?

'I ain't so sure we're doin' right to leave her alone with Lulie,' the older man grumbled as they climbed back into the 14-year-old Chevy after quarter-pounders at the local McDonalds. 'You know she ain't bright.'

'She'll do what we tell her,' the younger man insisted. 'I promised her I'd bring her a box of chocolate candy.' He grinned. 'Lulie will do anything for a box of candy.'

'Your brother know you been feelin' her up every chance you get?' His tone was skeptical.

'We share everything.' The younger man pulled to a stop at a red light. 'Shit.' But this was no time to be handed a ticket for a traffic violation. What did the boss say? 'Keep a low profile.'

'I think maybe you jes' wanna hang around out there at the cabin,' the older man accused. 'With Lulie.'

'What happens to Lulie after we let Sophie go? After the election? How do we know she ain't gonna talk?'

'Can't you figger out anything?' the older man scoffed. 'Lulie's gonna have a accident. A fatal accident.'

'But that don't seem right.'

'You an' your brother'll find yourselves another play-thing.' The older man shrugged.

'Maybe we oughta git rid of Sophie, too. Suppose she starts makin' trouble?'

'Sophie ain't seen us. How's she gonna identify us?' The older man grinned. 'And I'd jes' as soon not worry about tanglin' with them boys of hers.'

'I ain't sure we oughta let her loose after this,' the younger man began, then screeched in astonishment. 'Look at that!'

'Look at what?'

'That pick-up. Marty Mohammed's truck,' the younger man said in a surge of excitement. 'I thought the guys wuz handin' me a line about that reward. Marty and Joe guarantee to pay fifty thousand dollars for bringing in their old lady!'

'Where they gonna get fifty thousand dollars?'

'A loan on their house – from a bank! Wow!'

'Knock it off,' the older man ordered. 'We bring her in, we wouldn't live to spend one dime. You crazy, boy? We do what the boss says we do. Nothin' else.'

But $50,000, the young man thought. That was an awful lot of cash!

Twenty-Six

Karen sat at the edge of her chair, watched while Mike read her story. Anxious, insecure, she'd waited until the last moment to bring it in.

'It's great,' Mike said and yelled for Angie. 'You've hit on every essential point. Everybody in town is talking about Sophie's being missing. Of course, there are the creeps who insist she isn't missing.'

He paused as Angie strode into the office. 'You know what to do,' he said abruptly, extending the pages. 'Run with it.'

Now he turned back to Karen. 'Some folks are saying Sophie couldn't take the Arab-baiting any longer – she got the hell out. Some are blaming Hank Fredericks and *The Star* for building up anger against all local Arabs. Did I tell you?' He leaned forward, his face etched with contempt. 'This town is behaving so badly that some of our Arab-Americans – with children born in this country, speaking only English – are talking about going back to the Middle East. They feel safer over there!'

'That's the worst indictment this country could receive.' Karen stared at Mike in shock. 'Can we form a committee to talk to them? To persuade them to stay?'

'I'm talking to Doug about that. You know, get some legal information we can use. But first, we've got to figure out who abducted Sophie and where they're keeping her. Marty and Joe are out of their minds.' He paused worriedly.

'Joe's such a hothead – I'm scared he might make a bad move.'

'Can we bring in the federal government?' Karen asked. 'I mean, isn't there some deal about kidnapping being a federal offense?'

'Nobody in authority believes Sophie was kidnapped. There's that phony letter – and the money withdrawn from the ATM. They're all convinced she ran.'

'There's strong evidence she didn't write that letter – and the ATM withdrawal is a joke. Her pin was her name – easy to guess.'

'*We* know she was kidnapped – but how many others believe that?' He sighed in frustration. 'I talked with Doug a little while ago. He said we must decide whom we consider suspects – and watch their every move. *The Sentinel* will put up a fund to pay for a pair of private investigators.' He grinned. 'Those who'll work on a low pay-scale. We're not exactly thriving financially.'

'That list could go in two ways.' Karen's eyes held Mike's. 'It could be somebody caught up in the Arab-baiting craziness – or it could be somebody connected with the Fredericks campaign. Sophie was giving them headaches.'

'That's it,' Mike conceded. 'But we could be way off-base. It could be somebody with a personal grudge against Sophie. Like those property owners who want to sell to Sunshine when she's holding out. But we have to work fast, before they – whoever they are – take some desperate action.'

Karen felt a sudden coldness. Mike meant, 'Before they kill Sophie.'

Is she still alive? Can we find her in time?

Karen sat behind the wheel of her car and debated about going straight home. It was late. She was exhausted. But she was too wired to go to sleep yet. Call Lisa. She reached for her cell phone, punched in Lisa's number.

'Hi.' Lisa's greeting was cheery.

'You were expecting Howie,' Karen guessed.

'Not really. We just talked. I thought he might have had a last-minute thought. This is one of our singles nights. He's filling in tonight in the emergency room.'

'Too late for me to drop by?'

'Of course not. Come,' Lisa ordered.

Ten minutes later she sat with Lisa over coffee and reported on her day's activities.

'It's so awful not to know where Sophie is. Not to know if – if she's all right.'

'It's early in the game,' Lisa reminded. 'But until Sophie's found, that's all people in this town will be talking about. Howie says even patients in the hospital—'

'*The Star* is so rotten!' Karen grunted in exasperation. 'And both the radio station and the TV station have come right out and said they think this whole thing is a hoax.'

'The radio station and the TV station are selling air time like crazy to the Fredericks campaign,' Lisa reminded her. 'And *The Star* has been in Fredericks' pocket for years. Thank God, *The Sentinel* is on Sophie's side. And let's face it – there are a bunch of people sitting on the fence, not sure what to believe.'

'Doug says that Tony Mendoza's campaign funds are almost exhausted. His people are going to have to be very creative to win this election.'

'Karen.' Lisa took a deep breath. 'Are things better between you and Doug?'

'What do you mean by better?' Karen asked, startled.

'Have you talked about the early days? When you were both back in college?'

'No!' Karen hadn't meant to sound so explosive.

'He talked to me. He knows how close you and I are . . .' Lisa seemed to be choosing her words with care. 'What happened back in college – it wasn't quite what it seemed. He wants to talk to you – but I told him to give you some space. But maybe it's time.'

Karen felt a tightness in her throat. 'Not now,' she retreated. 'All that matters now is finding Sophie. I can't think of anything else, Lisa.'

Karen unlocked the door to her apartment, walked inside. It seemed so wrong to consider going to bed when Sophie was missing. She wouldn't allow herself to consider the worst. They needed to do more, she reproached herself, her frustration soaring.

The ring of the phone seemed unnaturally loud in the past midnight quiet. She hurried to respond, attacked by inchoate fears.

'Hello.'

'It's me,' Amy said with a note of apology. 'I heard your car, so I knew you hadn't gone to sleep yet. Have you heard anything about Sophie?'

'Nothing. But Mike tells me *The Sentinel* is setting up a fund to hire a pair of private investigators.'

'You know the nice Arab-American family that runs the laundromat on Edgemere Road? They've been here in town for close to forty years. I was talking to the grandmother – she comes to the Senior Citizens Center almost every day.'

'She teaches a knitting class at the yarn store,' Karen recalled.

'She told me today that they're thinking of going back to the Middle East. She said that her youngest son – who was born right here – said the family shouldn't live in a police state. Karen, that's what he visualizes happening here.'

'Mike didn't mention names, but he told me that was about to happen. He said he and Doug are talking about a committee to plead with them to stay.'

'I'm available,' Amy said. 'You hear more about a committee, I'm volunteering. I know *The Star* is a rag – but I read it so I can talk back. They're so convinced all the Middle-Eastern students attending college in this country are here to set up terrorist cells. They're pointing out that a lot of them are running home. Can't the jerks understand that we're scaring them out of their minds?'

'A few terrorists are posing as students,' Karen conceded. 'But most of the students are just eager to receive topnotch training in their chosen fields.'

'And we're doing ourselves a favor educating them,' Amy pounced. 'They go back home and improve their own countries, help make a dent in the poverty over there. And Karen, face it – it's poverty and illiteracy that breeds terrorism. Until we learn to help third world countries emerge from the dark ages, we'll have to cope with terrorism.'

'Sophie's such a fine person – this shouldn't be happening to her.'

'I'm going to bed now – but I don't expect to be doing much sleeping.' Amy uttered a long sigh. 'I just feel so damn useless.'

Off the phone, Karen walked into her bedroom. Not likely she'd do much sleeping tonight, either. She flipped on the lights. Her eyes sought out the red roses in a vase on her night table.

Lisa's words earlier in the evening ricocheted in her mind: '*What happened back in college – it wasn't quite what it seemed.*'

What was it then? What is Doug trying so hard to tell me? Every time my eyes meet his, I feel as though I'm about to enter a new world. But I'm afraid . . .

Twenty-Seven

In her nightie, Karen stood and peered through a chink in the living-room drapes. In early morning sunlight, Doug was walking towards her door. He'd left his car further down the road. He held a single red rose in one hand with an air of tenderness that set her heart pounding. He walked up the stairs and to her door.

In sudden alarm that she'd be seen, she released her hold on the drapes. Doug would be placing the rose right at the door – where she couldn't fail to see it. His morning mute plea for her to allow him to break down the wall between them.

She darted back to the bedroom. She'd see him in a little while, she reminded herself. He'd be at the Mohammed house. But she wasn't going there because of him, she told herself defensively. She had a job to do. What had Mike called her? A velcro reporter, attached to Marty and Joe until Sophie is found.

She went through the motions of showering, dressing, having a breakfast she didn't taste. Had anything happened in the course of the night? No. She would have heard.

It was early to go over to the Mohammed house, she thought – but she doubted that Marty or Joe had even slept. At least, be there for them. Stop by the newspaper store to pick up this morning's *Sentinel* and *The Star* on her way over.

With the two newspapers in tow – not bothering to read them at this point – she drove out to the Mohammed house.

Doug's car already sat in the driveway. Again, she remembered Lisa's words last night. *What can Doug tell me that will make everything all right?*

'Joe's out with the pick-up truck again,' Doug told her when she walked into the house. 'No word so far,' he replied to the question in her eyes.

'You have this morning's papers?' Marty strode into view.

'Both.' Karen held them out to him. 'I haven't read them yet.' He'd already seen her article that ran in this morning's *Sentinel*.

'There's coffee up,' Doug told her. 'I was just about to pour for Marty and me.'

'I'd love a cup.' Karen managed a wisp of a smile, avoiding meeting Doug's eyes. She'd lain sleepless most of last night – anxiety about Sophie alternating with unwary flashbacks of Doug and herself.

'Coming right up.' Doug headed for the kitchen.

'Son-of-a-bitch!' Marty's voice echoed with venom. He turned to face Karen. 'You didn't read *The Star*!'

'What's up?' Doug stopped dead.

'*The Star* is running Mom's letter – the one on the computer – and they know about the ATM withdrawal! How the hell did they get a copy of the letter?' Marty gazed from Doug to Karen. 'How could they know about the ATM withdrawal?'

'The DA's office,' Doug pinpointed. 'They want to make sure everybody knows. They're covering their butts for not investigating.'

'We'll give them a blistering answer in tomorrow's *Sentinel*,' Karen promised.

'But the circulation of *The Star* is four times as big as the *Sentinel*'s.' Marty was grim.

'We'll run a flier of today's article, and again tomorrow when Karen does a walloping reply,' Doug decreed. 'We'll have the campaign volunteers work with us on it.'

'Call Amy,' Karen suggested. 'She'll run with it.'

'Right.' Doug nodded in approval.

'I'll get the coffee,' Marty said. He paused. 'A couple of neighbors came over early this morning – one with home-made Danish and the other with a roast. They must have been in their kitchens at 5 a.m.'

'Marty, your mother has a lot of friends in this town,' Doug told him. 'They're anxious. They're praying for her.'

Emerging from exhaustion-provoked sleep, Sophie was conscious that she and Lulie were not alone in the cabin. She kept her eyes closed, feigned slumber. Lulie was talking with a man. One of the two who'd brought her here. She recognized his voice.

'Hey, baby, you be good to me and I'll be good to you,' he was coaxing.

'We can't do it here,' Lulie objected. 'Not with her sittin' just across the room.' She giggled. 'An' when you're wearin' that silly old ski mask. It makes me itch.'

'OK, OK,' he agreed. 'And don't you call me by name,' he exhorted. 'The way you do when you git all hot 'n' bothered.'

'She's real nice,' Lulie scolded. 'Why do we have to keep her here?'

'It's for her own good,' he said, breathing heavily.

'You said you'd bring me a radio,' she scolded. 'It's awful, just lyin' around here doin' nothin'.'

'It's in the box I put on the table – along with more bacon and eggs and bread. Oh, honey, I'm gonna make you feel so good when we git outta here.'

'When?' Lulie demanded. 'When do we git outta here?'

'When the right time comes,' he told her, and she squealed in sudden protest.

'You pinch too hard!'

'I got somethin' else for you,' he drawled. 'It's in the box, too. Some of them chocolate candies with the peanut butter centers.'

'Oooh!'

'I gotta go, Lulie. See ya in the mornin'. And if you're good, I'll bring ya somethin' else nice.'

'I'll be good. I'll be so good!'

'If she gives you any trouble, you call me, Lulie. You remember how to use the cell phone?'

'I remember.' A mixture of reproach and pride in her voice.

Lulie has a cell phone. Where is it? If I can get my hands on it, I can call 911 – leave it on so they can trace the call.

Sophie pretended to be asleep even when she and Lulie were alone. Then it was clear that Lulie had unpacked the box containing the radio. Hard rock shrieked into the silence of the cabin.

She opened her eyes. Lulie was off in a corner – dancing in a frenzy. *Where's the cell phone?*

'Joe's back with the pick-up,' Marty told Doug. 'My shift now.'

'Right.' Doug nodded. 'Keep it going.' So far no luck – but $50,000 was a lot of cash in this town. Somebody might crack.

Finishing up a lengthy phone call with a client, Doug reached for the mug of coffee that Karen had brought to him when she'd taken a break at the computer. Was he imagining that there was a crack in the wall between them? She'd said nothing about the rose at her door each morning – but she must realize it was from him.

The house phone rang. Doug rushed to respond.

'Hello.' Now he saw Karen hovering in the doorway.

'I figured you'd be there,' Mike began.

'I should have told you. We keep the house phone open. Let me call you back on my cell phone—'

'No need. Just get yourself over here. The investigators that *The Sentinel* is springing for – they'll be here in half an hour. I need you in on this.'

'I'll be right over,' Doug promised and turned to Karen. 'That was Mike. The two PIs the paper has hired are coming into the office in a bit. I'm running over.' He hesitated. 'Maybe you should be there, too.'

'I need to cover the phone,' she reminded.

'Joe can do that. Where is he?'

'Out in the backyard – chopping wood. He didn't hear the phone,' Karen surmised.

'Tell him he's on phone duty. We need to talk with Mike.'

Driving to *The Sentinel* office, Doug focused on Mike's latest effort to track down Sophie. Always in a corner of his mind was Lisa's exhortation to 'give Karen space.'

'Sophie's sharp. If there's any way she can reach out and give us a clue, you can be damn sure she'll do it.'

'I keep praying that she's all right,' Karen whispered. An unspoken fear that haunted them all.

'You have a lot of company,' Doug said gently.

They found Mike pacing about his office.

'So where are these guys?' Doug asked while he strode inside along with Karen.

'They'll be here in a few minutes. How're you doing with the story for tomorrow morning?' Mike asked Karen.

'It's finished,' Karen told him and reached into her purse for the pages. Later, Mike would read the article.

'OK, you two – what do we give these guys as leads?' Mike gazed from one to the other. A pugnacious attitude failed to conceal his anxiety.

'You've got two investigators—' Doug sat down, gestured to Mike and Karen to do the same. 'Send each off in another direction. One has to follow up the obvious Arab-haters. They're not hard to pinpoint.'

'There's so damn many of them!' Mike frowned. 'Go on.'

'All right – one guy is following the loud-mouthed Arab-haters. The other, instinct tells me, needs to look into this Sunshine operation. They're panting to buy four houses –

and only Sophie is holding out. And the rest of us—' Doug sighed. 'We've got to search our brains for an angle we're missing out on so far.'

Angie hovered in the doorway. 'The private investigators are here.'

'How do they look?' A wary glint in Mike's eyes.

Angie shrugged. 'Standard. It's too warm for trenchcoats, but they're into sunglasses.'

'Send them in,' Mike ordered. 'Let's get this show on the road.'

'You gettin' hungry?' Lulie was solicitous.

'Not more eggs.' Sophie made a pretense of shuddering. But her heart was pounding. She'd dug into the depths of her mind and had come up with a kernel of hope. *So it's way out in left field. It just might work.* 'I'm feeling kind of queasy.' She closed her eyes, groaned.

'Now, don't you get sick on me,' Lulie said in instant alarm. 'I ain't no good with sick folks. Maybe a cup of tea?' she asked hopefully.

'I've been on this special diet for years,' Sophie fabricated. 'If I go off it, I get awfully sick.' She clutched her stomach.

'Don't you throw up,' Lulie ordered. 'What kinda food do you eat – I mean, back home?'

'All I eat are veggie burgers and 7-grain bread. Before the health food store opened in town, I used to drive thirty-eight miles each way to buy them.' Sophie groaned. 'The last time I felt this way it was awful.'

'I'm gonna get 'em for you. Veggie burgers and 7-grain bread,' Lulie repeated. 'But don't you throw up.'

Sophie listened with simmering hope while Lulie carried on a repetitious conversation with whoever had left the cell phone for her use.

'Tell him to buy all the veggie burgers they have – if the store runs out, it might be a week before more come in,'

Sophie urged. 'And we don't know how long we'll be here.'
*Dear God, let Karen go into the health food store and get
my clue. This could be the lead they must be looking for.*

'You go over to that health food store and you buy a load
of veggie burgers and two loaves of 7-grain bread,' Lulie
said into the phone. 'Buy every veggie burger in the store
– we don't know how long we'll be here,' she repeated
Sophie's words. 'And do it fast. You didn't tell me she
might get sick on me!'

*I know I'm asking for a minor miracle – but it's all I
have. No way can I make a call on the cell phone. Lulie
keeps it in a drawer on the other side of the room. Let
Karen go into the health food store to shop. She's probably
out of things by the end of the week. Let her go in the health
food store and get my message.*

Twenty-Eight

Karen felt a wisp of hope after the conference with the two PIs. As Mike had conceded, *The Sentinel* couldn't afford the real-life version of Remington Steele and Laura Holt, but these two seemed sharp. Let them be sharp enough to track down Sophie's whereabouts.

'Are you going back to the house?' Doug asked as they settled themselves in the car.

'Right. The new article I'm working on is in Marty's computer.'

'I feel guilty eating the food Marty and Joe's neighbors bring in,' Doug confessed, backing out of the parking area.

'Maybe we could pick up dinner at some takeout place?' Karen said and stopped dead. She saw recall in Doug's eyes. Back in college they'd often had dinner in her dorm room or in the apartment Doug shared with two other students. Often they'd shopped at the health food store right off campus.

'That's a great idea.' His eyes were making ardent love to her.

'OK.' She switched her gaze to the strip of road ahead. Disconcerted by the unspoken words between them. 'Shall we try the health food store?'

'Sounds good to me.'

Doug parked before the health food store. He reached into his wallet for a bill.

'This one is on me,' she said. That would make it sound

as though they were sharing just a business arrangement. But the atmosphere declared otherwise.

Karen paused for a moment at the sight of one of the posters about Sophie posted on a store window, then hurried inside. She exchanged a few words of greeting with the friendly clerk. The owner wasn't here this evening. She walked back to the refrigerated section to make a choice. All these years later she remembered Doug's favorites. They'd start with veggie burgers, she decided, then add on.

She paused before the section where normally there would be a pile of veggie burgers. Not one package. This was a staple – shame on the store for running out of them. She checked the other refrigerated areas, made choices, headed for the check-out counter.

Why am I making such a production of choosing for our dinner? Nothing's changed between Doug and me. Except that I'm falling apart inside at being with him this way.

'You're out of veggie burgers,' she told the clerk with a wry smile.

'Oh, you just missed them,' the clerk apologized, ringing up Karen's purchases. 'Some man came in and took twelve packages – our whole inventory. I guess he has a bunch of health-conscious kids to feed.'

'Maybe next time.'

With her parcel in tow, Karen returned to the car.

'The store seems to be doing well.' Karen avoided Doug's eyes. 'I guess we have a lot of fellow travelers.' *Why did I say that? Linking us together.*

To break the silence that fell between them, Doug began to talk about the investigators, what leads there were for them to follow. Karen was grateful that only brief comments were required of her. She was agonizingly conscious of Doug's closeness – of her feelings for him.

They saw Marty driving up before the house as they approached. Joe was coming out to replace him.

'Any calls?' Marty called to Joe.

'Nothing,' Joe called back.

'Another tough night coming up for Marty and Joe,' Doug said compassionately as he and Karen approached the house.

Sophie hadn't slept in her bed since Tuesday night – and this was Friday evening, Karen thought in anguish. Even per police regulations she was missing – except that the police believed she had run away on her own volition.

'Will you be around to cover the phone if I'm not here?' Marty asked Doug when he and Karen walked into the house.

'I can be,' Doug told him. 'What's up?'

'I was thinking maybe it'd be a good idea for me to go out with Joe. You know, keep an eye on folks reading the sign. Maybe somebody is interested but scared. If I see somebody like that, I could leave the truck and try some persuasion.' He reacted to Doug's automatic unspoken question. 'Gentle persuasion.'

'Go with Joe,' Doug encouraged. 'I'll stay around.'

Karen went to the kitchen to prepare dinner for Doug and herself. She glanced up with a start when Doug walked into the kitchen. 'Everything's up. We can sit down and eat in a few minutes.' *Why am I rattling on this way?*

'Karen, there's something I must tell you,' he said with sudden urgency. 'I came back here nine years ago to tell you – but you were gone. I was stupid, incredibly naive . . .'

She stood as though frozen in space while he told her how he'd been hooked into marrying Candy. 'Before we met.' He told her about the lost baby that wasn't his – and about the divorce.

'Why didn't you tell me?' she whispered. 'Why did you run away like that?'

'I was in shock. It was though my whole life was being zapped away. Karen, there's never been anybody but you. I tried to tell myself I could forget, live my life alone – and then I walked out into the night and there you were—'

197

'I saw you, too.' Tears blurred her vision. 'I felt so terrible that you hadn't come to me. That I was being thrown aside with a cold phone call. I felt those months together had been a lie.'

'I wanted to tell you before, but Lisa said I mustn't rush you—' He reached to pull her into his arms. 'Karen, take me back into your life.'

'Oh, Doug, yes! Yes!'

Karen and Doug sat together on Sophie's sofa – her head on his shoulder, her hand in his. She felt suffused with guilt that she could feel such happiness when Sophie was missing.

'We can't expect anything much to happen with the investigators in the next twenty-four hours,' he warned, squeezing her hand in comfort. 'But—'

'Doug—' All at once her mind was clicking at top speed. 'I think we may be missing something.'

'Missing what?' But he, too, was at full alert.

A picture was leaping into her mind. Sophie sending them a message, hoping they'd connect this. 'I told you – there were no veggie burgers in the health food store.'

'Honey, we survived that,' he protested gently.

'You don't understand, Doug!' Her words tumbled over one another in her haste. 'The clerk in the store was astonished that somebody – I think she indicated it was a man – came in and cleared out the whole dozen that been on the shelves earlier. Normally people don't buy that many!'

'You lost me—' Doug was bewildered.

'You know how Marty and Joe tease Sophie about her obsession with veggie burgers. Somebody who bought that dozen in the health food stood could be holding Sophie!'

'Karen, you're fantasizing.'

'I know this sounds crazy – but just suppose Sophie is giving them a hard time – and they've decided to pamper her. Doug, maybe that's her message to us!'

Doug shook his head. 'That's far out.'

Karen sighed. 'You're right. I'm so anxious I'm reaching out for anything—'

'We have to focus on any lead,' he agreed, 'but it has to have some validity.' His right eyelid quivered, betraying his own anxiety. 'Otherwise, we could waste precious time.'

'It was a weird suspicion.'

But now he seemed ambivalent. 'I suppose we ought to follow anything that could be a possibility.'

'Fate does strange things.' Karen's eyes clung to his. 'I wouldn't be here today if fate hadn't kept me home the morning of September 11th. Perhaps fate sent me into the health food store right after somebody walked out with the whole inventory of veggie burgers. Giving us a lead to Sophie's whereabouts.'

In sudden resolution, Doug pulled Karen to her feet. 'We can't afford to ignore the weakest lead. Even if it seems absurd. Let's go back to the store and ask questions.'

Approaching the store, they spied the clerk – the one who'd been on duty when Karen had shopped. She was about to lock the door. Karen threw open the car door and stepped out before Doug had pulled to a full stop.

'Hi,' Karen said breathlessly. 'I'm so glad we found you here—'

'You just made it – I stayed late to rearrange some shelves.' Now she appeared solicitous. 'Was something wrong with what you bought?'

'No, everything was fine. But you said somebody bought a dozen veggie burgers just before I came in. Do you know who it was?'

'He'd never been in the store before.' The clerk hesitated, her eyes curious. 'Is it important?'

'It could be very important. Well, there's just a very slight chance,' Karen admitted, 'but it might lead to our finding Sophie Mohammed.'

'Oh!' The clerk frowned in concentration. 'I don't know him,' she said with regret. 'But I've seen him around town.

With that sweet little retarded girl who lives in the trailer park.'

'Do you know her name?'

'No, I'm sorry.' The clerk seemed troubled that she couldn't provide this information. 'I hope you find Sophie. She's a wonderful person.'

'Thanks for the tip. We'll follow it up.' With a hasty smile Karen darted back to the car. 'Doug, let me call Lisa on your cell phone.'

While she punched in Lisa's number, she told Doug what she'd learned.

'Hello.' Lisa's voice – warm and friendly, expecting a client – greeted her.

'Lisa, we need some help. There's a young retarded girl at the trailer park. Do you know her?'

'Oh, do I! That's Lulie Johnson. The family is on my client list. There was talk of child abuse a few times. And it's awful the way the parents just ignore her. With five other younger kids to keep track of, they let her roam around on her own too much. I keep expecting her to show up pregnant.'

'Lisa, we think one of her boyfriends may have Sophie. Can you help us track him down?'

'Honey, anybody who offers Sophie candy or cookies is her current boyfriend.'

'So, who's been giving her candy or cookies these past few days?' Karen prodded.

'Let me ask around,' Lisa said. 'Maybe I can come up with a name.'

'Lisa, get on it right now,' Karen pleaded. 'Sophie could be running out of time.'

Twenty-Nine

Lisa left her car in the parking area and walked towards a cluster of teenagers at one side of the trailer park. She knew two of the girls – clients of her agency.

'Hi, Glenda,' she called. Glenda and her friend were instantly wary. 'I'm looking for Lulie,' she explained. 'Have you see her around this evening?'

'Not for two or three days.' Both girls giggled. 'Lulie wanders off every once in a while.' Their eyes spoke volumes.

'She has a new boyfriend?' Lisa pretended indulgent conspiracy.

'Oh yeah.' Glenda grunted in distaste. 'That creepy Cal Henderson.' *Cal and his brother and father live in the trailer park.* 'Who else will go out with him?'

'What do they do?' Lisa asked as though amused by this combo.

Glenda and her friend exchanged more giggles. 'What do you think they do? When they ain't fishin'. Cal and Bart are always braggin' about what terrific fishermen they are.'

'If you happen to see Lulie, tell her I was asking about her,' Lisa said casually. 'See you around.'

She hurried back to her car, called Karen on her cell phone.

'Hello.' Karen answered urgently.

'Karen, Lulie's running around with Cal Henderson. I know, he's in jail again awaiting arraignment. But his brother Bart isn't. Try to locate Bart.'

'So Lulie is among the missing,' Doug summed up when Karen was off the phone. 'Probably with Bart. Who likes to fish—'

'Do you suppose Bart and Cal have a cabin somewhere – where they go to fish?' Karen's heart was pounding. 'Is Sophie in that cabin?'

'You read my mind.' Doug's eyes glowed with hope. 'Let's track down Mike, talk to him.'

Their first phone call told them Mike was still at the newspaper. They rushed over, were ushered into his office.

'Tell me you've got some good news about Sophie.' Mike's quizzical gaze moved from Doug to Karen. 'All I'm hearing is that the polls show Fredericks eating away at Tony's lead.'

'We're not positive,' Karen hedged, 'but we think we may be on to something important. About where Sophie is being held.'

'Sit down and talk.' Mike leaned back in his swivel chair, propped his feet on a pulled-out desk drawer, and listened to Doug report on what they'd discovered.

'You could be way wrong on this trip,' Mike warned. 'It sounds like desperate people trying to make a desperate rescue.'

'We know that, Mike,' Karen admitted. 'But it's all we have thus far.'

'So what do you want from me?' Mike looked from one to the other.

'We need to know if Cal or Bart or their father owns a cabin in some isolated area around here,' Doug said.

'You can't get into property records at this hour of the night. They're closed – you know that.'

'We're hoping you'll have some contact that'll get us into those records,' Karen said. 'This evening. Mike, Sophie's life may be at stake. We can't afford to wait until tomorrow.'

Mike deliberated for a few moments, then reached into

a drawer, pulled out a small black book. 'I can call in a favor,' he acknowledged. 'But I'm going to look like a horse's ass if this goes nowhere.'

Karen and Doug sat in tense silence while Mike made three phone calls. Now he leaned back with an air of exhaustion. 'We'll be met in twenty minutes. But it's going to be a real drag to try to find out if one of the Hendersons owns a cabin somewhere around here. OK.' He rose to his feet. 'Let's get cracking.'

Three hours later Karen, Doug and Mike still sat at a table in the room where Weston property records were stored. Bleary-eyed, Karen focused on the book before her. How many years could they go back? They had no way of knowing when one of the Hendersons might have scraped together enough money to buy a cabin.

'We might be here till morning,' Mike predicted. 'I'll run out and pick up coffee for us.'

'Wait.' Doug's voice was electric. 'I've got something!'

On either side of him, Karen and Mike leaned forward to peer at the listing that had captured Doug's attention.

'Almost eight years ago, Jud Henderson – Cal and Bart's father – bought a cabin out by the lake,' Doug told them.

'That was right after Hank Fredericks won his first term of office,' Mike remembered. 'Jud was supposed to be a gofer in Fredericks' campaign. That must have been a fancy payroll for Jud Henderson to have bought a cabin. Even a dinky one like this – judging from the price tag.'

'Let's notify the police.' Karen was already on her feet.

'No,' Doug rejected. 'The Chief's in Fredericks' pocket – they'll screw this up. I'm going out there! I'll line up Marty and Joe.'

'Better not,' Mike cautioned. 'Marty and Joe are too uptight. They might do something crazy.' Mike exuded a sudden glow. 'Hey, I haven't followed a big story myself in maybe twenty years. You and I will go out there, Doug.'

'That could be dangerous!' Karen was terrified.

'Cal's in jail. And thousand to one Bart and Jud have drunk themselves into a stupor with cheap wine. I'll take any bets that Sophie's there alone with Lulie.' Mike was on his feet.

'You don't know that,' Karen hedged. 'Bart and Jud could be out there guarding the cabin. With arms. What about the two PIs?'

'No time to track them down. Doug, you and I can handle this. I have a gun permit.' Unexpectedly Mike chuckled. 'A few years ago I had some threats against my life. I keep a gun in the night table beside my bed. First stop, my house.'

'I'm going with you,' Karen insisted. Mike stared at her in reproach. 'This is my story,' she said with an air of defiance. 'I'm not dropping it now.'

'I don't know.' Doug sounded uneasy.

'I know where the cabin is,' she reminded him. 'Take me along – or I'll follow you.'

'Maybe Karen can be useful,' Mike plotted. 'I've got a very simple plan.' He hesitated. 'Of course, we don't know if Sophie is out there in that cabin. And we don't know if Bart or Jud will be hanging around. Karen, you throw a rock through a side window to attract the attention of anybody inside. I'll break down the door, rush in like NYPD Blue. Doug, you follow me – unless I yell for you to get out. In case somebody is there with a gun.'

'Mike, this sounds like a bad TV show,' Karen said, worrying.

'It's the only show in town.' Mike slammed shut the book he'd been checking. 'Let's get this stuff back where it belongs. Then we hit the road.'

Karen huddled on the back seat of the car while Doug and Mike plotted their unfamiliar path. No traffic at this time of night. The only sounds those of animals in the wooded areas that flanked the road.

She felt a coldness unrelated to the night chill. Had she propelled Doug and Mike into a dangerous situation? Her fault if something terrible happened. Should she try to persuade them to turn around – forget this probably absurd venture? The knowledge that Mike carried a loaded gun was unnerving.

'It's the next right, Doug.' Mike was emphatic. 'I used to come out here years ago to swim in the lake.'

'It's so damn dark,' Doug complained, hunched over the wheel. The night sky was overcast – not a star in the sky, not a sliver of moon to be seen.

'It's just another mile or so,' Mike soothed, and it seemed to Karen that Doug stepped hard on the gas. 'We don't have to make it in twenty seconds.'

'No sign of life around here,' Doug noted but he slowed down.

'You don't want to encounter a frightened doe on the road,' Mike told him. 'We're close,' he said with sudden urgency. 'We're lakeside now.'

Karen glanced out the window, shivered at the closeness of the road to the night-dark water. She'd always been fearful of driving at the water's edge. Tonight it seemed especially menacing.

'Pull over to the right,' Mike told Doug. 'We'll walk the rest of the way.' He leaned forward. 'There's a light about two hundred feet ahead!'

'A car?' Doug was wary as he drove to the side of the road and parked.

'No car that I can see. That's a kerosene lamp in a cabin.' Mike turned around to Karen. 'You stay here in the car until we're sure it's safe.'

'What about your plan? I'm to throw a distracting rock through a window while you storm the front door.' She was deliberately flippant.

'I gave it some thought – it's too dangerous.' Mike was brusque. 'Move up front.' He and Doug were emerging into

205

the cold darkness. 'If you see lights behind you, honk three times, then drive on.'

'What about you and Doug?' Karen was unnerved.

'If we see trouble coming, we'll walk.' His calm, somehow, exacerbated her own anxiety. 'Just get out of here if you see another car approaching.'

Karen settled herself behind the wheel – her eyes already fastened to the rear view mirror. But they'd walked no more than 40 feet, she estimated – lost as they were in the darkness – when doubts assailed her. *If there's trouble, I want to be there with them.*

She left the car, followed them – stumbling at intervals in her haste. There they were, just ahead. She took a deep breath of relief. An eerie stillness all around. No sign of another soul other than themselves.

'Wait for me.' Her voice sounding abnormally loud in the stillness.

'Karen!' Doug was upset. 'You should have stayed in the car.'

'And miss all the excitement?' *How can I sound so cool when I'm terrified?*

'There it is.' Mike's voice was electric. 'Knowing the Henderson creeps, I can't see them patrolling the cabin when they're sure nobody's around.'

'How can they be sure?' Karen demanded.

'Because they're stupid asses,' Mike barked, then lowered his voice because every sound seemed super-loud out here. 'OK, keep it quiet.' They were approaching the cabin. 'Karen—' He paused, bent down to pick up something. 'I want you to throw this rock through the side window at the count of ten and—'

'Suppose there's a screen?' Karen interrupted. Throwing a rock would be a warning of people around.

Mike squinted at a front window. 'No screens,' he judged. 'Count at this pace.' He demonstrated. 'You throw the rock, provide a diversion. I'll break down the door.' He grinned.

'So I look out of shape. Believe me, I can do it.' He reached at his waist for the gun he'd stashed there. 'Doug, keep behind me. Remember what I said – you beat it if I yell for you to get out.'

'Now?' Karen asked, clutching the large rock in both hands.

'Now,' Mike said. 'Start counting.'

Pushing her way through overgrown bushes, Karen headed for the side of the cabin. Counting under her breath. She approached the one window at this side – still counting. She looked inside – through a flimsy curtain. *Sophie's here!* 'Nine – ten—' With a rush of strength she threw the rock through the window.

Simultaneously she was aware of the door being broken down and of shrill screams. With a burst of speed, she charged around to the front of the house. Doug was unlocking the pair of handcuffs on Sophie's wrists. Mike was trying to calm a terrified young girl. She must be Lulie, Karen told herself.

'Lulie, it's all right,' Sophie tried to calm her. 'These are my friends. They won't hurt you.'

'Cal told Bart we had to keep you here,' Lulie sobbed. 'You're real nice – I like you. But Cal said we'd be in real trouble if we didn't keep you here. He said the Mayor – he'd be awful mad.'

The other three exchanged a swift glance of comprehension. 'Well now, would he?' Mike drawled.

'You're going to be all right, Lulie,' Sophie reiterated while Doug freed her ankles. Mike breathed out in relief as Sophie crossed to pull Lulie close. 'We'll make everybody understand.'

Mike turned to Doug, pulling his cell phone from a pocket. 'Call the police. They need to pick up some guys on a kidnapping charge before they find out what's happened and hit the road.'

'And it sounds to me as though Mayor Fredericks won't

207

be running for re-election—' Doug was punching in numbers on the cell phone. 'Now isn't that a shame?'

'And you know what else?' Mike was smug. 'What do you want to bet the Sunshine people are going to stop playing games and offer Sophie and her friends market value for their houses? Because they know damn well Mayor Tony Mendoza won't play games with them.'

'You'll come home with me,' Sophie told Lulie. 'You'll stay with me tonight. And in the morning – like we were talking about – we'll bake fresh bread together.' Sophie turned to Doug, mouthing words. 'You'll talk to the juvenile authorities? Lulie's not responsible for what happened.'

'I'll handle it,' Doug promised. 'And Lisa's familiar with the family's problems – she'll work with me. Lulie will be OK.'

'Not a bad night's work.' Mike grinned in triumph. 'All right, let's get this show on the road. The car's nearby. First stop, the police station. But you and I, Karen – we don't hang around there. We've got to set up a new headline for tomorrow morning's *Sentinel* – which might be a little late in coming out. And you've got a front-page story to write. And not much time to write it—'

'She's real pretty,' Lulie said with a touch of awe, watching as Doug pulled Karen close. 'Is that her boyfriend?'

Mike chuckled. 'Yeah, I think it's safe to say he is.'

Thirty

The atmosphere in the police station was super-charged. No scandal as traumatic as this had ever hit Weston. And in a few hours the entire town would know.

Bart Henderson and his father were now behind bars – along with Cal. It would only be a matter of time before the Mayor and his henchmen – who'd ruled the town for almost eight years – joined them. Kidnapping was a federal offense. They were, as the Police Chief phrased it, 'in deep shit.' The FBI would take over. And nobody could guess how many other heads would fall before the case was closed.

Doug stifled yawns as he prepared to leave – simultaneously exhausted and exhilarated. It had been a rough night – but Weston would be reclaimed by the good citizens of the town.

'Doug, you understand?' The Police Chief – summoned from his bed an hour ago – seemed uncomfortable. 'We know we have to bring in the Mayor. But we'd rather do it a couple hours later.' He managed a weak grin. 'He's not going anywhere.'

'No problem,' Doug reassured him.

Cal and Bart – though their father had at first been reticent – spilled out an ugly tale of corruption and crime: *'Hey, if we didn't do what the Mayor said, he'd finish us off. He's gettin' real desperate about the election. He said we gotta stop Sophie Mohammed from goin' out and stealin' voters.'*

Doug walked out into the early morning. The sky a rose-pink, waiting for the sun to burst above the horizon. In the car he hesitated a moment in debate. Tony would still be asleep. But yes, wake him up. Tell him what had been happening. Great news should be savored as soon as possible.

He punched in Tony Mendoza's home phone number, waited with a whimsical smile for the jarring intrusion to bring a response.

'Hello.' Tony's voice was foggy with sleep. *But he won't mind this wake-up call.*

'Tony, I don't think you have to worry any more about competition from Hank Fredericks.' Doug launched into a tight account of what had occurred in the last few hours.

'Great! And thank God, Sophie's all right,' Tony said. 'In a way we can say she'll be winning the election for us.' He laughed. 'We minorities have a way of getting around, don't we?'

'Tony, this country is made up of minorities,' Doug said. 'The only full-class Americans are the American Indians.'

Off the phone Doug debated about his next move. Go over to *The Sentinel*. Mike and Karen would probably still be there – waiting to see this morning's edition come off the press. And they'd want to be brought up to date. They'd stayed briefly at the precinct, had left to take Sophie and Lulie home, then on to *The Sentinel*.

Doug stopped at a local diner that opened at 5 a.m., ordered coffee and Danishes to go. With package in tow he headed for *The Sentinel*. He found Karen and Mike in Mike's office – the first of the morning's newspaper spread before them.

'I've brought sustenance,' he said lightly, depositing the package on Mike's desk. His eyes scanned the headline: 'MAYOR AND CLOSE ASSOCIATES GUILTY OF FRAUD AND KIDNAPPING'. 'Wow!'

Over coffee and Danishes they discussed the impact of these revelations on the town.

'We'll have clean government after nearly eight years of Fredericks' dirty shenanigans,' Mike said with satisfaction. 'We know whoever's brought in to replace Fredericks on the ballot won't have a chance. Does Tony know?'

'Oh, yes.' Doug was focusing now on reading Karen's story. 'This is terrific.'

'With the FBI in on the case,' Mike pointed out, 'the story will be spread around the whole state. It might even hit the supermarket tabloids: "THE GOOD FOLKS OF WESTON, NY, RECLAIM THEIR TOWN".'

Karen swigged down the last of her coffee and sighed. 'I'm beat. I could sleep around the clock.'

'Take the woman home,' Mike said with mock gruffness. 'She left her car somewhere around.' He gestured eloquently.

'I'll take her home,' Doug agreed.

They drove to Karen's apartment in serene silence. Karen's head on Doug's shoulder.

'Honey,' he asked gently as he parked in her driveway. 'Are you asleep?'

'No.' Her eyes sought his. A radiance there that belied her sleepiness. 'Not at a time like this.'

'You said you were beat.' He felt a surge of anticipation at what he read in her eyes.

'I've got my second wind,' she whispered. 'Doug, I'm so glad I came home.'

Karen stirred, aware of a voice calling to her. Doug's voice, she realized, and smiled without opening her eyes.

'Are you planning on sleeping the day away?' he chided tenderly. 'We've got things to do.'

She opened her eyes. Clad in a towel, fresh from a shower, Doug hovered above her.

'Hi.' She was suffused with recall of her reunion with Doug. For a little while – early this morning – her apartment had been a corner of heaven.

'Go shower,' he ordered. 'I'm making breakfast.'

She glanced at the clock. 'Oh Doug, it's almost one o'clock!'

'You're not working today. It's allowed.' His eyes made passionate love to her again.

'I love you,' she whispered.

'I love you, too. What would you say to a Thanksgiving weekend wedding? Then my folks can fly in from Arizona with a duel purpose.'

'I think it would be beautiful.' After all the empty years she and Doug had found each other – and nobody would ever separate them again.

'Go shower,' he ordered again. 'I'll have breakfast on the table by the time you're done. Oh, Mike called. We're scheduled for a top level meeting at campaign headquarters at 2 p.m. Mike and Tony set it up.'

'OK.' She tossed aside the light quilt. 'What's up?'

'We'll find out when we get there.'

'There must have been an uproar in town this morning when *The Sentinel* got around – and the phones must have been ringing off the hook.' Karen's face lit up. 'People have something to think about besides hounding Arab-American citizens.' But now her face showed concern again. 'Doug, what about Lulie? She seemed so sweet, so vulnerable . . .'

'She's with Sophie. I'll go into court to have her cleared of the business with Sophie. Lisa said she'd work to have Lulie taken into a group home for "special children" that's been set up in a nearby community. She's been trying for that for almost a year, but the parents have managed to nix it. Lisa said that won't happen this time.'

'Doug—'

'You're stalling on showering,' he joshed.

'Was this just about the election?'

'No.' His air of levity evaporated. 'Remember, Cal and Bart Henderson beat up Marty – badly enough to send him to the hospital – because of his Arab heritage. And Hank Fredericks used that rage to propel them into keeping Sophie out of action until after the election. That and a chunk of cash,' he surmised.

'All these people with this horrible – unjustified – rage – how do we wake them up?' Her mind darted back to what she'd read and heard about the Japanese-American internment camps during World War Two, and the horrendous McCarthy period. 'How can we do this?'

'I think that this morning's *Sentinel* – along with the reports on radio and TV about Sophie's ordeal – may be a wake-up call.'

'Mike will keep the story alive on the front pages for weeks,' Karen predicted. 'We'll *make* people understand.'

'Fredericks will be replaced on the ballot, of course. Tony's a shoo-in.'

'But will this vendetta against the Arab-Americans in town continue?'

'No.' All at once Doug was adamant. 'We won't let that happen.'

Thirty-One

K aren and Doug hurried from her apartment to his car. 'We're going to be late.' Karen felt an insistent trickle of guilt. 'You should have awakened me earlier.' But it was only a tender rebuke.

'We'll be on time,' Doug insisted. 'Well, perhaps a couple of minutes late. Is this what I'm facing for the next fifty years?' he joshed. 'A wife who's one of those characters with a compulsion to be on time?'

'You spoke with Mike and Tony?' Karen sought for reassurance as they settled in the car.

'Honey, they're right along with us in our thinking. We have to make this town realize that every American – regardless of ethnic background – is an American. Tony's making that a cornerstone of his campaigning for these final days. Mike's talking with the School Board about sending in a pair of psychologists to talk to the kids about the diversity of this country – and how every ethnic heritage must be respected.'

'And everybody needs to understand that Islam is a religion of peace and good will,' Karen said softly. 'The attack on September 11th was the work of fanatics. Terrorists. We all must understand that, Doug.'

Arriving at campaign headquarters, they knew by the number of cars in the parking area that most of those summoned to the meeting had arrived.

'We're late,' Karen moaned.

'A minute or two,' Doug comforted.

They strode into campaign headquarters – immediately aware of the electric atmosphere. The news had spread, Karen guessed. The election was still 16 days away, but everyone knew that Tony Mendoza would be Weston's next mayor.

'Hi!' One worker, then others called out in triumphant greeting as Karen and Doug hurried back to the office Tony shared with Doug.

Breathless in their rush, Karen and Doug approached the office – where a dozen people sat on folding chairs brought in to accommodate them.

'And let me remind you,' Tony told those gathered around his desk as Karen and Doug appeared, 'that we wouldn't be so sure of this election without the efforts of Doug Madison and Karen Hunter. Because of them a corrupt mayor and certain members of his administration have been unmasked. We can reclaim our town.'

'And remember Sophie Mohammed,' Karen added – in a corner of her mind startled yet again by her aggressiveness. 'If Sophie hadn't figured out a way to get a message to us, we wouldn't have found her. They meant to keep her out of circulation until after the election. They realized the minority vote – which she was after, very effectively – could swing the election in Tony's favor.'

'I say, let's give a "welcome home" party for Sophie.' Amy Lansing hovered in the doorway with a dazzling smile. 'Let's offer the town's apology to all our Arab-American friends.'

'*The Sentinel* will sponsor the party,' Mike picked up, 'in conjunction with the Mendoza campaign. And every Arab-American family in this town will be our guest of honor.'

Karen and Doug were led to a private corner table at The Elms – Weston's most elegant restaurant, located in a landmark white colonial at the edge of town. The entire lower floor had been opened up to form a spacious, lushly carpeted dining room. Floral damask drapes hung at the tall, narrow windows. Every table draped in white tablecloths topped by a vase of fresh flowers.

'It was a great idea to come early,' Doug whispered, glancing about the room. 'It's almost as though this is our own house.' Only two other tables were occupied.

'I was afraid if we had a late dinner, you'd fall asleep before dessert. And I know what you'll order,' she laughed in sudden recall, the years melting away. 'No matter how fancy the restaurant, you always order chocolate ice-cream.' She paused. 'Do you still order chocolate ice-cream?'

'I'm more sophisticated now.' His foot sought hers under the table. 'I order chocolate mousse.'

A waiter arrived to take their order. They argued in high spirits about the merit of the salmon versus the tuna.

'You have the poached salmon and I'll have the grilled tuna,' Karen told Doug with mock sternness. 'Then we can share.'

The waiter observed them with pleased indulgence. *He knows we're in love. He suspects we'll be marrying. Perhaps we'll have a small wedding reception here.*

'It's a lovely place,' Karen said when their waiter left them.

'We couldn't afford anything like this back in college.' A reminiscent glow in his eyes. 'Remember all the Chinese takeouts and the pizzas?'

'We have so much making up to do—'

'And we'll have a wonderful time doing it.' His hand reached across the table for hers. 'I was so proud of you at the meeting this afternoon.'

'I was proud of you,' she said tenderly. 'You've done so much for this town. People here know that.'

'I thought that was all there was to be in my life. And then I walked out of that house across the way from Amy Lansing's – and there you were. I knew I'd die if I couldn't bring you back into my life.'

216

'It was only half a life for me without you.'

'Welcome home, my love.'

'It's wonderful to be home.' Tears stung her eyes, but they were tears of joy.

'This morning while you slept,' Doug confided, 'I called Mom and Dad out in Arizona to tell them about us.' He laughed at her start of astonishment. 'And you know what Mom said? "Well, it's about time!"'

'Then I guess that makes it official,' Karen said softly.

I'm not an onlooker of life any more. I'm participating. Doug – and this town – have made me understand that we must care about what happens to others in this world. We must help to build a better tomorrow.